'There's more,' she said, and he gripped the railing tight. 'Some ground rules. No L word. No marriage proposals. No cohabitation.'

'What's left?' His voice held a bitter edge as he braced himself for her answer. Her cool dismissal of the things he wanted most wounded like barbs tearing his flesh.

'Good times, Campbell. I don't know how long for. Let's just take each day as it comes.'

PRACTISING AND PREGNANT

Dedicated, doctors, determinedly single—
and unexpectedly pregnant.

These dedicated doctors have one goal in life—to heal
patients and save lives. They've little time for love but
somehow it finds them. When they're faced with single
parenthood too how do they juggle the demands and
dilemmas of their professional and private lives?

PRACTISING AND PREGNANT

Emotionally entangled stories of doctors in love
from Mills & Boon® Medical Romance™

As a twelve year old, **Amy Andrews** used to sneak off
with her mother's romance novels and devour every
page. She was the type of kid who daydreamed a lot
and carried a cast of thousands around in her head, and
from quite an early age she knew that it was her destiny
to write. So, in between her duties as wife and mother,
her paid job as a paediatric intensive care nurse and her
compulsive habit to volunteer, she did just that! Amy
lives in Brisbane's beautiful Samford Valley, with her
very wonderful and patient husband, two gorgeous kids,
a couple of black Labradors and six chooks.

The Midwife's Miracle Baby is Amy Andrews's
first novel for Mills & Boon® Medical Romance™

THE MIDWIFE'S MIRACLE BABY

BY
AMY ANDREWS

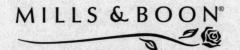
MILLS & BOON®

To Karen, midwife extraordinaire, for helping my daughter
and recently my nephew into the world. You are a truly special person
with a truly special gift.

And to the RBWH Birth Centre for a magnificent job.

*All the characters in this book have no existence outside the imagination
of the author, and have no relation whatsoever to anyone bearing the
same name or names. They are not even distantly inspired by any
individual known or unknown to the author, and all the incidents are
pure invention.*

*First published in Great Britain 2005
Harlequin Mills & Boon Limited,
Eton House, 18-24 Paradise Road, Richmond, Surrey TW9 1SR*

© Amy Andrews 2005

ISBN 0 263 84302 5

*Set in Times Roman 10½ on 12 pt.
03-0405-49245*

*Printed and bound in Spain
by Litografia Rosés, S.A., Barcelona*

CHAPTER ONE

CLAIRE took a deep breath and pushed open the solid oak door. Here we go again, she thought. Six men sat around the matching oak table in the boardroom. Their conversation stopped. It appeared they'd started their departmental meeting without her.

'Ah, Sister West, do join us.' Dr Martin Shaw, St Jude's Obstetric Director, pushed back his cuff and looked at his watch.

Claire felt the scrutiny of six pairs of eyes as she prayed that her legs, which suddenly felt as wooden as the furniture in the opulent room, would move her to the indicated seat.

Anger sparked them to life as she reminded herself she had a job to do. This posse of six thought they could ruin one year of her hard work? Determination flushed her cheeks and glittered in her rich, cinnamon-colored eyes. They really ought to know her better than that by now.

She noted her placement at the head of the table and wondered nervously if they'd reserved it to honour her or interrogate her.

'I don't believe you've met our new consultant,' said Martin. 'Sister West, meet Dr Deane.'

Claire bristled at Martin's formality. They had known each other for years, surely he could use her first name? Claire wouldn't have minded so much if she hadn't been absolutely certain that it was Martin's way of keeping her in her place. You nurse, me doctor.

Unfortunately, only a few years off retirement, he was, like so many doctors of his generation, clinging to the formalities of a bygone era when doctors had been gods and nurses merely their handmaidens.

Well, this is a new millennium, she wanted to yell. Move on or move out of the way. Normally she ignored his irritating habit of using her full nursing title, but Claire was already annoyed that she had to be here at all. Unfortunately the hospital board, in its wisdom, thought she might be able to make a difference.

'Campbell. Please, call me Campbell.'

His rich voice invaded Claire's thoughts, dragging her gaze to him. So, this was the man that had driven the hospital grapevine into overdrive! His reputation with the ladies had preceded him. Apparently he was quite the man!

Claire had been so nervous she hadn't even noticed Campbell Deane. Staring at the newcomer, she couldn't think why. Even seated, she could tell he was tall. Tall and broad-shouldered, his impressive bulk dominating the chair. In fact, dominating the whole table.

And young, too—relatively speaking. She judged him to be in his mid-thirties. At least two decades younger than the other men in the room.

But it wasn't her impression of his size that drew her interest, it was his hair. Thick and longish on top with a tendency to flop in his eyes, and very definitely red. Not carrot red, more subtle and peppered with golden highlights that hinted at a fondness for the beach.

It reminded her of a long forgotten ex-fiancé. OK, so Shane's hair had been a different shade of red. Deeper. But the way it drew her gaze was the same. The way it tempted her to run her fingers through it…the same. Great! As if she needed that distraction right now!

His eyes were green and beneath the faint shadow of stubble at his jaw was skin that had obviously seen its share of boyhood freckles. Although considerably faded now, they afforded a tantalising glimpse of his younger years.

As Claire reached across to shake his proffered hand she felt a tingle of apprehension. Something told her she should avoid all physical contact with this man. Just as she should have with Shane. Some lessons in life were too painful to repeat.

'Claire,' she said automatically, as the warmth of his hand enclosed hers. And then something happened. For the briefest moment as his skin touched hers she felt… energised. Like he'd transferred his warmth into her body, raising her temperature a degree. He smiled at her and his eyes glittered like emeralds in sunshine. She knew he'd felt it, too.

She withdrew her hand abruptly and sat, wiping her still tingling palm on her white uniform. Her mind spun. She didn't need this now. She really didn't.

She needed to focus on her objectives for this meeting. She couldn't afford to be distracted by a man who vaguely reminded her of someone else. She thought about Campbell Deane's reputation in an effort to refocus her thoughts. One ladies' man in her life had been more than enough!

So, he was attractive. But the only thing she needed to know about him now was his opinion on alternative birthing practices. The word was he had a more modern approach, but was it really the case? Would he be as difficult to reach as the others? Would he be old school, too? Would he be an enemy or an ally?

The meeting got back on track and Claire pushed thoughts of Campbell Deane out of her head as she perused the agenda. She grimaced and fought her rising irritation. She was last. Item number ten—Birth Centre. The board may have forced their hand, but this group of men weren't going to smooth the way.

She frowned at her watch and resisted the urge to drum her fingers on the table. They may be able to sit around and chat for hours but she had a job to get back to. Nobody else would do it for her while she sat in this room. Claire didn't have the luxury of registrars and residents. She wasn't asking them for much, just a bit of support.

Claire was aware she was considered radical. She thanked her lucky stars this was the twenty-first century and not medieval times. Back then midwives had been regarded with suspicion and often accused of witchcraft. She had a feeling they would have burnt her at the stake years ago. The thought seemed absurdly funny in such a modern setting and Claire smiled to herself.

She looked up and noticed Campbell Deane staring at her, a small smile playing on his full lips. He winked at her and Claire could sense his interest. She dropped her gaze back to the agenda and decided to ignore him.

It was time to emit her famous 'not interested' vibes. Because she wasn't—absolutely not. And even if she had been, the rekindled memory of Shane and their messy break-up ten years ago served to remind her that men were not part of her life equation. That was the way it had to be and Claire had accepted it a long time ago. She wouldn't let an attractive stranger ruin her focus.

The meeting dragged and Claire's impatience grew. She tapped the foot of her crossed leg lightly on the table leg and didn't care how rude it appeared.

Campbell's persistent gaze was unsettling. She didn't have to look at him to know he was staring. She could feel it. The intensity of his scrutiny was almost a physical caress. She doubted he'd heard any of the discussion. He certainly hadn't contributed.

All Claire could do was continue to pretend he didn't exist. She deliberately kept her eyes averted, staring directly at Martin with what she hoped was rapt attention. She shook her head slightly and the heavy curtain of her dark bob swished forward, obscuring some of her face. It was a move designed to hobble his interest. She had to put him off. She just had to.

Despite this, there seemed to be an energy channelling between them that was hard to ignore. Claire could stand his attention no longer. It was doing strange things to her body. She felt like she'd been for a light run, instead of sitting idly. It was totally ridiculous—she'd just met the man!

'Excuse me, Dr Shaw.' She interrupted him in mid-flow.

'Yes, Sister?' He peered over his glasses at her, obviously startled by her intrusion.

'I'm sorry to interrupt.' Claire knew he was unused to interruption. 'I really can't stay for much longer. Do you think we could discuss the birth centre now?'

She was pushing her luck but Claire didn't really care at this precise moment. She had to get out of this room as soon as possible. Before she did something absurd, like stare right back at Campbell Deane.

'Yes, all right, Sister. You have the floor.'

Claire was relieved to stand and stretch her legs. She took a moment to collect herself. A lot was riding on how she presented her case. It was imperative she hold onto her temper.

'Gentlemen, I think we all know why I'm here. I know that opening up a birth centre here at St Jude's hasn't been popular among the obstetric staff. But the hospital board has approved—'

'That's only because it was raised at a board meeting with no obstetric representative, Sister West…by you, I understand.'

Claire stalled at the polite accusation. She couldn't deny

it. She had deliberately waited for the most opportune moment to present the proposal to the board. Claire had known they'd run with it once the idea had been raised, especially as it was extremely cost-effective for the hospital. Money talked.

'Nevertheless…' she smiled nervously, very aware of Campbell Deane's quiet stare at the periphery of her vision '…this project has taken a lot of work and the centre is virtually ready to open. We've accomplished a lot at a negligible cost to St Jude's. All we need now is for one of you—or more,' she joked, yeah right, 'to agree to provide a referral service for our clients. As part of the protocol we've developed, we need an obstetrician to see our ladies first, assess their level of risk and then refer them to us if they fit our criteria.'

'Sister West, I believe you know how we feel about this issue.'

'Yes, Dr Shaw, but the board feels otherwise.'

'What the board says means nothing if you can't get an obstetrician on your team,' he pointed out, and Claire felt her anger boil at his smugness.

'You forget, Dr Shaw, the reason we're offering this service is consumer pressure. The women of Brisbane want a birth centre.'

'What? So they can give birth hanging from the rafters?'

Claire ignored his sarcasm. The obstetric staff had been sent copies of the birth centre philosophy, including alternative birthing positions. His exaggeration was typical.

'Shouldn't women be allowed to give birth hanging from the rafters, if that's how they feel most comfortable?' she asked with saccharine sweetness.

'And if something goes wrong?'

'That's the beauty of the centre,' she said, clinging to the slender thread of her patience. 'For the very small percentage of women who need it, medical attention is only seconds away. It's the best of both worlds—a home birth in a major hospital. That's all we want. It's not some conspiracy to make an obstetrician get down on his hands and knees to deliver a baby.'

'A most unsuitable position,' tutted one of the other doctors.

'There are other positions much more amenable to giving birth besides the stranded beetle,' Claire snapped. She'd seen too many women forced to give birth lying on their backs. She could feel her patience wearing thinner.

'It's the easiest,' he replied angrily.

'No, it's the most convenient for doctors.' Claire took some deep breaths, trying to rein in her anger. 'Look, gentlemen, some women want natural births with no drugs and no or minimum medical intervention—'

'You have something against medical intervention?'

Campbell Deane's rich voice broke into the debate. She spun and looked at him, surprised that he'd decided to add his two cents' worth. Oh, hell, she thought. He's one of them.

'No. Not if it's necessary.' Her voice sounded weak and flustered, even to her own ears. She cleared her throat, determined to inject the passion this subject always engendered in her. 'I do, however, oppose the medicalisation of what is, after all, a very natural process. Women have been giving birth since time began without the complex equipment and procedures we can't seem to do without today.'

'Women used to die, too.'

'Yes, some women did,' Claire agreed. 'That's why we have obstetricians.'

'I believe St Jude's has a natural birth rate of seventy-five per cent. That's very good, Claire.'

About to launch into another diatribe on her pet subject,

she halted abruptly at the use of her name. Not just that he'd used it but the way he'd said it. It slipped slowly down her back, as if he'd stroked his finger down her spine. She felt her skin feather with goose bumps.

'Ah…yes,' she floundered, trying to collect her thoughts. He smiled at her, an encouraging smile, and she tried not to stare at his mouth as she picked up her train of thought. 'But that still leaves twenty-five per cent of women who are having some form of medical intervention, and half of them are Caesareans.'

'You don't believe in C-sections?' he queried.

'Not unless they're necessary medically.' Claire wanted to scream. Why was it so hard to get through to these people? Campbell Deane might be younger than his colleagues but he seemed to be tarred with the same brush. 'In this day and age women can and should have a choice over how they deliver their babies. They want an elective Caesarean? Fine. An epidural? Fine. Truckloads of drugs? Fine. I just don't think women are given an informed choice. For example, how many of the twelve per cent would have progressed to a C-section if they hadn't had a whole gamut of medical intervention first? We all know it tends to have a spiralling effect. And C-sections done for obstetric convenience only are deplorable.'

'Convenience? Such as?' asked Martin testily.

'Golf games,' she snapped.

To Claire's absolute surprise Campbell threw back his head and laughed. His glorious hair flopped back, the golden highlights catching the afternoon sun streaming through the window behind him.

'I hardly think that's fair comment,' Martin blustered.

Claire knew Martin played off a three handicap. You needed to spend a lot of time on the greens to be *that* good.

'I'm sorry,' said Claire, annoyed at having let her temper sidetrack her from the issue. 'That was uncalled for.'

'I should think so,' Martin muttered.

'You're missing the point,' Claire said, with barely concealed impatience. 'It's all set and ready to go. Whether you agree with it or not, it's a done deal. The birth centre is here to stay. What the board wants, the board gets.'

'I'm sorry, Sister West.' Martin shook his head. 'We've discussed this in great detail. Now, I can't speak for Dr Deane, but I know the rest of us agree that we're not comfortable with such a role. It's a big responsibility. Our medical insurance skyrockets every year as it is.'

Claire looked around the table as all of them, with the exception of Campbell, nodded in agreement.

He remained silent. His stare seemed to be weighing her up. She had known that this meeting wasn't going to be easy, but she'd also been sure she'd be able to sway at least one of St Jude's six obstetricians. It was a board initiative. It had been funded and set up—they couldn't refuse. But they had.

Claire felt the heat of her anger flare and rage inside her. 'Well, thank you, gentlemen,' she said with icy sarcasm, gathering her papers, 'for nothing. I don't have time to stand here and beat my head against a brick wall. I guess we all know where we stand.'

Quelling the urge to glance Campbell Deane's way one last time, Claire turned on her heel and marched out of the room. She knew it was childish but she slammed the door after her for good measure.

'Wow.' Campbell expelled a long whistle, stopping about the same time as the windows stopped rattling. She had been magnificent. Obviously passionate about her cause and ready to do what it took, take on whoever it took to see her plans come to fruition.

Not that he'd actually heard a lot of what she'd been saying. It had been difficult to concentrate when so much of the blood that usually dwelt in his brain had found its way to another part of his anatomy. He hadn't had such an instantaneous response since that time when his eighth-grade maths teacher had bent over to help him and he'd had a glimpse of her lacy bra.

If anything, this time was worse. She hadn't had to flash any underwear, just one impassioned diatribe, and he was almost dizzy from the lack of oxygenated blood to his brain. He noted the other men's laughter and was secretly amused by their relieved expressions. Sister Claire West has left the building!

'She married?' he asked. They laughed again, louder this time. Yep—definitely more relaxed now.

'I don't think you're her type.'

'Too old? Too young? Too obstetrician-like?'

'Too male,' said Martin, and the group laughed again.

The answer confused him momentarily. Campbell felt his hackles rise as realisation dawned.

'It seems she likes to wear comfortable shoes,' someone else said with a snigger, amused at his little joke.

'Oh, I get it.' Campbell's icy voice cut through their little-boy laughter. 'Because she doesn't fall at our feet and fawn all over us, she's a lesbian?'

'So the rumour goes,' agreed another, and grinned conspiratorially.

Campbell thought of his sister Wendy and how rumour and innuendo had dogged her because of her sexual preference. Such archaic attitudes made him angry. It flared in his eyes as the other men laughed, oblivious.

'Knocked back every available doctor in the hospital. A

couple of not so available ones, too.' Martin laughed. 'She was involved with a guy years ago but I know for a fact that she lives with a woman now—Mary. I think that's her name anyway. Shame really. Beautiful girl. Damn good midwife, too. Just doesn't know her place.'

'Well, now, that won't do, will it?' Campbell's voice was caustic.

'I say, old chap,' blustered Martin, the mirth slipping from his face. 'Just a bit of harmless fun.'

'Excuse me, gentlemen,' Campbell said politely. He pushed back his chair and grasped it firmly in case the growing urge to wipe the superior looks off their faces suddenly overwhelmed him. 'I have other business.'

Claire steamed into the deserted staff dining room and made herself a cup of coffee. It was too early for afternoon tea so she had the large room to herself. Good. At least she'd be able to hear as she silently berated herself. In half an hour the noise level in the room wouldn't allow for mental self-flagellation.

She flicked impatiently through her notes as she sipped the hot drink. Neat, concise, calm, reasoned. Absolutely nothing like her performance in the boardroom. She shut the folder in disgust. Try insulting and inciting. She'd blown it! Her agenda had been to flatter a few egos and gently persuade. Instead, she'd gone in with a caustic tongue and a sledgehammer.

Where they would go from here, she really had no idea. It would have to go back to the board and they would have to apply pressure. Claire had no doubt that eventually the obstetricians would have to back down. The board could be an immovable force when it wanted something badly enough. Fortunately, it believed in the birth centre.

But it all meant more time. As if the process hadn't been

slow enough already. This latest development delayed things further. Damn them, Claire thought as she stared into the murky depths of her coffee. Her eyes were a matching colour as she worried her bottom lip.

Unbidden, Campbell Deane's face entered her mind—again. His red-blonde hair, his green eyes, the intensity of his stare. The way he said her name.

'Claire.'

His voice startled her, causing the remainder of her coffee to swish perilously close to spilling into her lap.

'May I sit down?' He gestured to the seat opposite.

Still smarting from what had happened in the boardroom and irked by the way her hands were trembling, Claire wasn't feeling very charitable.

'Something wrong with all the other tables in this joint?'

Despite her deliberate rudeness, he threw back his head and laughed, and Claire was reminded how he had laughed at her golf *faux pas*. She felt her scalp tingle.

'You're not sitting at them.' His laughter sobered to serious contemplation.

Claire felt her breath stop in her throat as their eyes locked and held. Cinnamon brown drowning in sea green. She pulled her gaze away with difficulty.

'It's a free country.' Claire shrugged her slim shoulders. She had to be nonchalant, cool. She couldn't let him see that somehow he'd created a chink in her defences. He mustn't find out.

'I'll do it,' he stated, pulling out the chair and sitting down.

'What?' She eyed him dubiously.

'I'll be the admitting obstetrician.'

Claire's first reaction was to reach over and kiss him. But her ever-present sensible side cautioned her against wild impulses.

'Why?' she asked, trying to keep her bewilderment at this sudden turn of events in check.

'Because the birth centre philosophy is everything I believe in. I'd love to be part of it.'

'Didn't sound that way in the boardroom.'

'I was playing Devil's advocate.' He shrugged. 'I wanted to test your conviction. See how passionate you were about your cause. Very, as it turns out.'

Claire blushed. She'd certainly left nobody in that boardroom in any doubt about how passionate she was about the centre. She regarded him seriously. Dared she hope? Could Campbell Deane be trusted?

'You won't be popular,' she stated.

'I've never really cared for what other people think.'

He shot her such a dazzling smile Claire wanted to reach for her sunglasses. He was flirting, she realised with dismay. Claire had been flirted with enough to recognise the signs. Oh, dear. This wouldn't do at all.

'You're not doing this to…be popular with me?' she asked.

'Would it work?' His green eyes sparkled with humour.

'Definitely not. I don't date.'

'Oh? And why is that?'

'Didn't they tell you about me? About my sexual preference?' Claire watched as Campbell valiantly tried to swallow his mouthful of coffee instead of spluttering it all over her crisp white uniform. 'I'm not stupid, Campbell. I know what people say about me.'

'I guess I didn't expect you to be so open about it,' he mused, facial contortions now under control. 'So, is it true?'

'What do you think?'

'I hope not.'

Claire held her breath. A surge of energy had charged between them again. The surroundings faded away as her gaze locked with his. 'And if I am?' Claire couldn't stop the question tumbling from her lips. She blushed as his gaze zeroed in on her mouth.

'It would break my heart.' His voice was little more than a whisper.

She registered his preposterous statement but still didn't seem to be able to drag her eyes away from his hungry gaze on her mouth.

A burst of raucous laughter heralded the first people arriving for their afternoon tea. Claire quickly pulled herself back, the spell broken. How had she got so near? He seemed to exert some kind of magnetic pull she couldn't resist.

'This is an entirely unprofessional, inappropriate conversation,' she stated briskly, gathering her crockery together and rising to leave.

'Absolutely. I agree,' he said, also rising and falling into step beside her. 'Perhaps we could have a more appropriate conversation another time. Over dinner maybe?'

'I don't do dinner,' she said primly.

'Lunch?'

'No.'

'I suppose breakfast is out then?' he suggested cheekily, and her step faltered at his implication. She stopped before she tripped.

'You're wasting an awful lot of time on someone whose not supposed to be interested in men.'

'I think you are.'

'Really? And how do you know that?'

'The way you looked at me before…we definitely shared a moment back there. No one interested in women would look at a man like you just looked at me.'

'Oh, really? An expert on sexual behaviour, are you?'

'Nah. My sister's a lesbian. Trust me—she's never looked at a man in that way. Ever. Not even as a baby.'

'OK, so I'm heterosexual. Don't tell anyone. I'd hate to ruin my reputation,' she quipped, and walked away.

'So, who's Mary?' he called after her, catching up easily.

'Mary?'

'The woman you're allegedly living with.'

It was Claire's turn to laugh now. The absurdity of it all gave her a fit of the giggles.

'You don't live with a woman called Mary?'

'No, that piece of information is one hundred per cent correct. Mary West. My mother.'

'Ah.' Campbell laughed, seeing the funny side. 'In that case…'

'Look,' she said, stopping again. 'Thank you for your support with the birth centre. I appreciate it more than you can ever know. But…if it's going to come with strings, then you should know, I won't play that game.'

'No strings, Claire. I promise.' He laid his hand on his heart.

She rolled her eyes and continued on her way, walking quickly. To her dismay he continued to keep pace with his long-legged stride.

'Can't a guy just ask a girl out?' he cajoled.

'Like on a date?'

'Yes.'

'I told you already—I don't date.'

'What, never?'

'Now you're catching on.'

'I'm going to keep asking until you say yes.'

'Why?' She stopped abruptly. Exasperation strained her voice.

'Because from the moment I saw you today, I knew you were the only woman for me.'

For a moment she wondered if he'd pulled out a stun gun and shot her with it. She couldn't remember ever being lost for words. 'Don't be ridiculous. You...you've only just met me,' she spluttered.

'Don't you believe in instant attraction? Love at first sight?' he asked. The smile that warmed his face seemed to detract from his crazy statement.

'No,' she croaked emphatically, her feet finally responding to the frantic messages from her brain. Get out of here now. Run like the wind. Campbell Deane was certifiable.

Claire shook her head to clear it as she walked away. Her coal-black bob swayed like a piece of satin around her head as it swished from side to side. If she hadn't heard it with her own two ears, she wouldn't have believed it. Campbell Deane had to be insane. She should have enquired if he'd been taking his medication lately. It was patently obvious that he'd missed a few days.

Worst of all, she was going to have to decline his offer to join the birth centre team. It would do nothing for their fledgling reputation if their admitting obstetrician was as nutty as a fruitcake.

She pushed the button for the lift as Campbell caught up with her.

'I'm scaring you away.'

'You're crazy,' she hissed.

'Only for you.'

'Campbell.' She turned to him, exasperation changing her eyes to a turbid brown. 'This is the most ridiculous conversation I've ever had, but let me set you straight anyway. Whatever fanciful notions you're entertaining, I suggest you forget them immediately. My interest in you is purely professional. I'm grateful to you for coming to the rescue of the birth centre. But even if I were the dating kind, I certainly wouldn't go out with a man who talks like he's just escaped from the loony bin. I also wouldn't date someone who seems to have a bigger reputation than Casanova.'

'Ah.' He smiled, unperturbed. 'You don't strike me as someone who listens to gossip.'

'The whispers about you were pretty loud.'

'Look, sure, I've had my share of relationships.' He shrugged nonchalantly. 'All mutually satisfying and all mutually ended. But I always knew that when I found the one, my Casanova days would be over.'

The one? Yeah right. That sounded familiar. She'd been here before. 'Well, that's great. I hope you find her. But I'll tell you something for nothing—I am not the one. I am not interested. Don't waste your time on me.'

'So you don't feel anything for me, then?' he asked with a completely fake crestfallen look.

'Gratitude.'

'Gratitude?'

'Respect. I respect that you took a chance instead of following the crowd.'

'That won't keep me warm at night, Claire,' he teased.

'Buy an electric blanket,' she quipped, and leapt into the lift, grateful for its timely arrival.

Claire almost screamed when he followed her in. Her heart pounded painfully in her breast. Despite her protestations, she was desperately trying to quash an excited flutter taking hold of her body. His persistence was flattering on a level Claire didn't want to acknowledge. It had been a long time since a man had persevered. The wall she had built around herself was thick with thorny brambles. It took a brave man to even attempt to hack his way through.

'Claire—'

'Shh,' she hissed, desperation taking over. 'Don't talk.'

'It's not going to go away, Claire.'

'How old are you, Campbell?'

'Thirty-five.'

'Too old to be carrying on like a lovesick adolescent.'

'Are you ever too old for that?' he asked quietly.

Claire shut her eyes and sighed deeply. She'd read something in Campbell's eyes. An emotion that was blindingly honest. The lift reached her floor and Claire's relief was palpable. Once again Campbell followed her out.

'Why are you following me?' she muttered, annoyed by his dogged persistence.

'I was hoping for a tour of the birth centre. Surely that's not too much to grant your knight in shining armour?'

Claire suddenly felt churlish. Of course he would want to see it. Now who was being unprofessional? Claire kicked herself for not having offered sooner. It might also have given them something else to talk about. 'It's an excellent idea,' she agreed, shooting him a grateful smile.

Grateful to be back on familiar ground...even if she was walking it with Campbell Deane beside her.

CHAPTER TWO

TRYING to ignore the man walking next to her on the way to the centre was impossible. Damn it all! Why couldn't he be old and fat and balding with bad breath and an even worse toupee? Instead, the man who turned out to be her saviour was as sexy as hell, with hair and green eyes you could fall into. The fact that he also resembled someone who had hurt her badly ten years ago was a whole other distraction.

Claire was very confused. How had this man got under her skin on such short acquaintance? Was it the Shane factor? No. This reaction was completely new. Not even with Shane had she felt so instantly and acutely aware of a man. Whatever the reason, Claire knew it all added up to one thing—danger.

Pushing aside her confusion and the prickle of unease she could feel all the way up her spine, she concentrated on the joy at showing off her 'baby'. Confidence and pride added a spring to her step.

'Here we are,' she announced, as she retrieved a set of keys from her pocket and opened the double swing doors. The sign above said, WELCOME TO ST JUDE'S BIRTH CENTRE. He preceded her and Claire couldn't contain the thrill of excitement that always hit her when she walked through the doors. It was her dream, the culmination of a year's work.

'This place used to be one of the postnatal wards until it was shut down a few years ago. We've taken over the first two bays on either side of the corridor. It's my hope that one day the centre will need the entire ward area.'

'You're ambitious.' He smiled. 'I like that.'

'No, not really,' she continued, 'I just want to see the beds made available. We already have a waiting list. I don't want to see our numbers restricted by space constraints.'

Claire opened the door to the first birthing suite. It was spacious, taking up an entire bay which once would have held six beds. A large, low, queen-sized bed was neatly made up with a bedspread that matched the bright, attractive curtains. Beside it a mobile crib, complete with a warming blanket, was ready to receive a newborn.

There was also a sofa which converted into a double bed and next to it a bar fridge, as well as tea- and coffee-making facilities. Behind it was a bathroom with a shower cubicle and a toilet. Against the far wall was a bathtub. Two trolleys stood against available wall space. They had covers that matched the curtains to disguise their medical purpose. One was for linen and the other carried equipment, which was used at the moment the baby entered the outside world.

Every effort had been made to create a homey atmosphere. It was as far removed from standard hospital accommodation as you could get.

'As you can see, there's plenty of room for whatever support team the couple wishes. The double bed allows for partners to stay with the new mum if they want.'

'What's the policy on siblings?'

'If that's what the parents want, that's fine, as long as there is a support person solely to look after the older child or children.'

He nodded his approval and Claire beamed.

'You planning some water births?' he asked.

Claire laughed. 'Can you see the board agreeing to that?

I thought I did a good enough job getting them to agree to the centre.'

'I've delivered a few. In the right circumstances, it's a wonderful experience.'

Claire was becoming more impressed with Campbell's grasp of modern birth practices. Perhaps he wasn't insane after all. Professionally he seemed completely *compos mentis*.

'Water births would be fantastic, but maybe down the track a bit. One step at a time. I really pushed for the baths. Water is too often overlooked for pain relief. So many women find the warmth and buoyancy an incredible help. The plumbing was the most expensive part of the conversion.'

'It's been really well thought-out. The room looks... peaceful.' He followed up his compliment with a broad grin.

It had been exactly what they had hoped to achieve. So often babies were born into bright, noisy environments. Part of the centre philosophy was to create a peaceful, harmonious atmosphere. Claire soaked up his positive comments like any mother proud of her baby. She felt weak from the full force of his smile.

'The other room is a mirror image of this one,' she said, indicating the closed door. 'Across this side,' she said, walking into the room opposite, 'is our office area.' The room held three desks. 'Two desks for the four midwives and one for our receptionist. And in here...' she opened a large built-in cupboard near the door '...is the resuscitation trolley and other medical equipment in case of emergency. The laughing gas is kept in here also.'

Campbell pulled the trolley out of its alcove. He removed the green cloth that covered the top and checked everything. She watched his large hands run over the array of first-line emergency drugs, the selection of breathing tubes and masks. His long fingers opened the drawers and checked the oxygen and suction hanging off the side of the trolley.

'Everything's here I would ever need in an emergency,' he said approvingly, and Claire felt like she had passed some kind of test.

'The other room is a staffroom-cum-commonroom. We'll use it to eat our lunch or whatever, and clients can use it to make themselves a cuppa while they're waiting to be seen. We're also planning on running our own antenatal classes. This room will be perfect for that.'

It was spacious enough. There was a sink with a jug and coffee and tea things and a microwave near the entry. A round table with four chairs stood nearby. Over by the window were a couple of comfortable lounges. A bookshelf on the wall held a variety of midwifery and birth-related books and journals.

'You've done a great job, Claire.' His easy compliment massaged her ego.

'It wasn't just me. Four of us worked on the project and set the centre up. I was just the one delegated to deal with all the red-tape stuff.' She grimaced and screwed up her nose.

'Because…you're so good at it?'

Claire laughed. 'No. Because it was my idea and that was all the reason they needed to make me do it. You should meet the others in the next few weeks.'

'How about you have dinner with me tonight and fill me in on how you envisage the centre will run?'

Claire wasn't fooled by his innocent smile. Same motive as before, just disguised in a different wrapper. Who was she kidding? If her life were at all normal then she'd have jumped at the chance. He was, after all, a very attractive man. But there was so much about her life that was complicated.

It was far easier to deny herself completely than to suffer the inevitable heartache. That was the mantra she lived by. Despite this, Claire felt a flutter in her chest that was an entirely new experience for her. Why? She hardly knew the man!

'Take a seat.' Claire indicated behind him. 'I'll fill you in now.'

He laughed but pulled up a chair anyway. Claire continued.

'Pregnant women, when they first make contact with the hospital, will be offered our service. If they decide it's for them, they'll have their initial consultation with you. If they're suitable, you'll refer them to us. All their subsequent appointments will be with us. We'll see them every four weeks until twenty-eight weeks, and then every fortnight until thirty-six and then weekly until they deliver. Same as usual. If they haven't delivered by forty weeks then you'll see them again to check everything's OK.'

'Right. I assume it's short stay? How long do they stay after the baby is born?'

'Twenty-four hours generally. Each case will be different, of course. It'll also be influenced by demand. If women wish to stay longer, they'll be transferred to one of the postnatal wards. The hospital's Community Midwifery Service will follow up the women who choose early discharge. Then we see them here again six weeks later.'

'Very good.' He nodded. 'But what about the birth? What pain relief do you offer? What's the procedure if complications develop?'

'We offer gas and pethidine, although we'd prefer to try alternatives first.'

'Such as?'

'Heat, massage, positioning, water. However, if the client wants something stronger, or if complications develop, we transfer them to Labour Ward. We continue to be their midwives and will still deliver their babies, and then they come back to the birth centre afterwards, depending on their level of intervention.'

Campbell continued to fire questions at Claire. She answered them in full.

'One more question, Sister West.' He smiled, his green eyes glittering with mirth.

'Yes?' she replied warily.

'Do you like Thai or would you prefer Indian?'

Claire groaned and rolled her eyes. 'Neither.'

'Italian?'

'I'm not going to go to dinner with you, Campbell. Quit asking.'

'I never quit. My mother says I'm the most stubborn person she knows.'

'Well, I think you've just met your match.'

'I'm not going to go away, Claire. I won't give up.'

'Always get what you want, huh?'

'No, not always. I've just never wanted anything so much before.' Campbell's pager beeped and he whisked it off his belt, frustration marring his handsome face. 'Saved by the bell, Claire West. I've got to go. Labour Ward needs me.'

Claire stood, grateful that he was finally leaving and that she'd be able to breathe properly again. He stood at the same time and suddenly their bodies were a whisper away from touching. She wanted to close the gap so badly, she had to look down to cover the surprising reaction his proximity had caused. Something was wrong—she'd known him for less than two hours! This shouldn't be happening.

'This isn't over.' The low timbre of his voice slid down

her spine as he pressed two fingers beneath her chin and raised her head. 'It's just the beginning.'

She held her breath and stood very still, watching his green eyes glitter with promise. And then he was gone and Claire sagged into the chair, relieved to be alone.

Well, his mother was right. Claire had never met someone so determined. If he pursued her as relentlessly as he had today, how long could she hold out against his resolve? Especially when she knew, deep down, that if the circumstances of her life had been different, she wouldn't have hesitated.

Claire couldn't deny she was attracted to Campbell, and it had been a long time since she'd felt that about a man. It had been a long time since she'd even been with a man. And many had tried. One or two had even been quite persistent. But despite their ardour, she'd been unmoved.

It had been easy to stick to her guns when the men in question had done nothing for her. But Campbell was a real enigma. Could she honestly say she was indifferent to him?

Claire shook herself. It didn't matter. She was still bound by her no-relationship policy and it was one she must adhere to, no matter what artillery he used to try and persuade her.

She might be appealing to him now, but Claire knew from bitter experience that initial attraction waned. She need only think of Shane to be reminded of that. Campbell didn't know it, but she was doing this for his own good.

'Ready for the last patient, Campbell?' Sister Andrea Marshall asked, poking her head around his office door. She'd been nurse in charge of Obstetric Outpatients for the last five years. She had been at St Jude's for as long as Claire, and they had done their midwifery training together.

He stretched and smiled at her, noting her keen interest.

She'd been flirting with him all morning. A month ago he wouldn't have hesitated but, since meeting Claire, all other women had ceased to exist. Still, her interest was flattering to his increasingly deflated ego. A harmless flirtation with a busty blonde was exactly the right medicine.

'Sure, Andrea, send her in,' he said, his mind distracted by the challenge Claire presented.

That she had been avoiding him, and quite successfully too, hadn't escaped his notice. Still, he was prepared to wait. All good things came to those who waited. Didn't they? And with the birth centre officially opened last week, Campbell knew she wouldn't be able to shun him for ever.

Andrea ushered in his patient and handed him the chart.

'Hello, Mrs Craven. I'm Campbell Deane. Congratulations on your pregnancy. Twenty weeks already.' He smiled and shook his patient's hand, noting the area of darkened pigmentation across her face, which was common in pregnancy and caused by hormonal changes.

'Call me Lex, please.'

'So, you're planning on having the baby here at St Jude's,' he said, flicking through the chart.

'Yes, Dr Deane, that's what I wanted to talk to you about.'

'Please, call me Campbell.' He'd never been comfortable with the blind reverence afforded to doctors. His mother had always taught him that respect should be earned. He didn't consider that what he did for a living automatically made him better than the next person. We're all just cogs in a wheel, his mother, a midwife herself, insisted. Besides, his four sisters, three of them nurses and one a GP, were always ready to cut him down to size should he let his position go to his head.

'I got a phone call last week from the receptionist at the

birth centre—I'm in! I'm so excited.' Her dark, wavy hair bounced as she laughed.

Campbell joined her, noting her glow of excitement. 'Well, congratulations again.'

'Thanks. I've really wanted to have my baby there ever since I heard about it.'

'Oh, yes? And why's that?'

'Well, I've read so much about active birth and I really like the philosophy. I've bought and borrowed every book there is on the subject. The whole concept of a birth centre is fantastic. Kind of like a home birth but with medical back-up if you need it.'

'I think we need to put you in charge of advertising.' He laughed. 'You sound like an ideal candidate. Have you thought about how you're going to cope with the pain?'

'I'd like the baby to be in the best possible shape when it arrives, so drug-free is my ultimate aim. I'll try all the alternatives first. But I'm flexible. You hear enough horror labour stories to know it's going to hurt.'

'Good for you. I think flexibility is definitely the key.'

'The receptionist said I needed to see you first and get a referral.'

'That's right, so let's do it. Hop up on the examination bed over there.' Campbell walked to the door and called to Andrea, who was sorting through a mountain of charts. 'Andrea's going to stay while I examine you. Blood pressure first.'

He pulled the cuff down from the wall and quickly took Lex's BP. 'Perfect,' he said, smiling. Next he asked her to slip her skirt down slightly so he could feel her abdomen. 'Sorry, cold hands,' he apologised in advance. What was it with hospitals? The air-conditioning always seemed set at freezing.

Campbell shut his eyes as he gently probed Lex's abdomen, feeling for her burgeoning uterus. He found the top and Andrea handed him a tape measure. He measured the distance from her pubic bone to the where his hand was. Twenty weeks exactly.

'Would you like to hear the baby's heartbeat?' he asked.

'Of course,' she said with a laugh.

Andrea gave him a hand-held Doppler. It was similar in appearance to a transistor radio. He squeezed a daub of gel on Lex's abdomen and turned the machine on. He fiddled with the volume control and turned it down until the noise was less jarring. Manipulating the transducer through the gel, he quickly located the steady *whop, whop, whop* of the baby's heart.

They were all silent as the noise filled the office. Campbell loved this part. The sounds of new life never ceased to amaze him. The miracle of it all. This was why he'd become an obstetrician. He grinned at Lex and saw the shimmer of tears in her eyes.

'What a beautiful noise,' he said.

'One hundred and sixty-four,' said Andrea, who had counted the beats.

'Excellent,' said Campbell, switching off the machine and wiping gel off Lex.

He left Andrea to help her straighten up, walking back to his desk to peruse her chart once more.

'Swabs are negative. Blood tests unremarkable. Haemoglobin good. Any foetal movements yet?'

'I've been feeling fluttering for a couple of weeks now.'

'Good,' he said, writing in the notes. 'Any concerns?'

'Nope.' She shook her head.

'All right, then. You can give the birth centre a ring and organise an appointment for four weeks.'

'Oh, thank you so much, Dr Deane…I mean Campbell. You don't know how much this means to me.' She jumped up and shook his hand vigorously. 'Actually, I think I'll go up there now. I haven't seen it yet and I can make my appointment while I'm there.'

'Good idea,' said Campbell, grateful for this golden opportunity. Look out, Claire West. Here I come. 'I'll walk you there,' he offered.

Lex Craven's excited chatter occupied most of Campbell's attention on the short walk. As they alighted from the lift on the fifth floor, Campbell listened less, becoming tuned into his body's anticipation. He could feel his heart thudding in his chest and echoing in his ears.

His stomach growled, reminding him that it was almost two o'clock and he hadn't had anything to eat since breakfast. Maybe he could persuade Claire to join him for some lunch? Nothing ventured, nothing gained.

He saw her the second he walked through the doors. She had her back to him, talking to a client, and he noticed the easy way she held her body when she didn't know he was around. She was too erect and straight when she talked to him. Like she was afraid that if she relaxed, even for a nanosecond, she might get too close.

He loved how her white uniform fitted her perfectly. It accentuated her lushness, flattering her curves and emphasising her cute derrière. It was a stark contrast to her rich olive skin and her midnight-black bob. Just watching her now, his fingers itched to feel its silky weight.

She turned to usher her very pregnant client to the door and spotted him. He watched with dismay as her clear brown gaze became muddied with caution.

'Campbell,' she said. 'This is a surprise.'

Obviously not a pleasant one, he thought. In fact, looking at her expression, he felt about as welcome as a venomous snake.

'I've bought Lex Craven for a visit. I've just given her a referral.'

Claire had to stop herself from breathing a sigh of relief. He was here professionally. She'd been very busy in the last couple of weeks, which, while tiring, had been advantageous. She'd seen him rarely and when it hadn't been avoidable, her excuses to take her leave had been completely genuine. No matter how brief their contact, she never felt in control of herself around him. He made her feel…clumsy. Claire was terrified of clumsy.

'How wonderful to meet you,' said Claire, greeting their latest client with delight, temporarily forgetting her Campbell-induced anxiety. 'Go on in and make yourself a cuppa,' she said, indicating the commonroom. 'I just need to have a quick word with Campbell.'

Campbell raised his eyebrows as Lex disappeared into the room. She wanted to chat? Was that good?

'Campbell, I'd like you to meet Shirley Miller, one of our clients.'

'A pleasure.' He smiled and shook her hand. He hadn't met her yet so his registrar must have seen her.

'Shirley's thirty-three weeks and her baby has just decided to go breech.'

'Bit of a swimmer, hey?' he joked lightly, and Shirley laughed.

'My other three have been breech until the last four weeks.'

Ah. Fourth child, he thought. That explained her very large tummy. He would have put her closer to term.

'Could you feel the position properly?'

'Pretty sure it's lying frank,' she said.

'Well, you've got a few weeks yet for the baby to turn.'

'Here's hoping,' said Shirley, and held up crossed fingers. 'I so want to have the baby here.'

'We'll cross that bridge if and when we get to it,' he reassured her. 'Did Claire give you some postures you can try at home to encourage the baby to turn?'

'Sure did. I'm going home right now, before the kids get home, to try them out.'

She said her goodbyes and they watched her leave the premises.

'She does understand she'll have to deliver in the labour ward if the baby doesn't turn?'

'Of course, Campbell,' Claire said testily, annoyed at her body's response to his nearness. 'Don't worry. I won't break any of your mates' precious rules.'

'No need to be so touchy,' he teased, his green eyes sparkling. 'I didn't make the rules.'

'I'm sorry,' she said. 'You're right. But one day, Campbell...one day I hope that we'll be able to offer all kinds of births here.'

'Amen to that,' he said, hand on his heart.

'Goodness, I can hear your cronies having apoplexy as we speak.'

He laughed heartily and his red-blonde hair flopped back. 'C'mon, Claire. Even you've got to admit that breech presentation is potentially much more complicated.'

'Potentially, sure. But you and I both know that Martin and his pals automatically think breech equals C-section.'

'You think trial of labour first?'

'Depends on the woman and the presenting part. There are too many variables. You can't treat them all the same, as Martin and co do.'

'They're just scared, Claire. Haven't you ever been scared?'

His question startled her. It was like he had seen right into her soul. Had she? About one thousand per cent more than anyone could know. She'd been scared for the last ten years.

'We…we're…not talking about me,' she stuttered. His astuteness was unsettling.

'Right.' He grinned. 'Shame…I'd much rather talk about you.'

'Me?'

'Us, actually.' Campbell watched as fear and confusion reflected briefly in her eyes before she masked them behind a shutter of wariness.

'Campbell.' She rolled her eyes and took a step away from him. She couldn't think when he was too close. 'I thought you'd given up.'

'Nope. Just haven't been able to track you down much.'

He stared pointedly at her and Claire felt her face warm. He knew that she'd been avoiding him.

'I've been very busy,' she said, sounding lame even to her own ears.

'Have you had lunch?'

'No.'

'Let me buy you some. I'm starving.'

'I've brought mine,' she replied stiffly.

'OK. I'll watch. I like to watch.'

Claire stared at him incredulously. Was he serious? His expression was far from it. He looked like raucous laughter was only seconds away. He was winding her up.

She rolled her eyes and smiled grudgingly. 'I'm going to show Lex around.'

'I'll wait for you at your desk.'

'Don't bother. I'm never going to agree to go out with you.'

'We'll see. Never say never.' He grinned and ducked away before she had a chance to protest.

Claire would have screamed out loud if it hadn't been

for Lex in the next room. She wanted to stomp her foot so badly, it itched. Suppressing her childish impulses, she went to join Lex.

She felt herself relax as she gave their new client the grand tour. She answered all Lex's questions and then went back to her desk to make an appointment. She ignored Campbell, who was poking around the office.

'I understand you're offering antenatal classes?' asked Lex.

'That's right. You start them at about twenty-eight weeks. They'll run every Wednesday night for four weeks. Would you like me to book you in?'

'Yes, please.'

Claire retrieved the booking diary from her desk drawer, ignoring a muscled thigh she could see in her peripheral vision as Campbell lounged against her desk. She pencilled Lex and her husband in to start in eight weeks' time.

As Claire bade her goodbye, Campbell joined her. 'See you in four weeks,' said Claire.

'Actually, I might see you tomorrow. I've got my ultrasound at ten.'

'Oh, what a shame you didn't get an appointment for today. Save you coming back again tomorrow.'

'It was the only one available this week, otherwise it was a couple of weeks' wait. Unfortunately Brian is away until next week so he's going to miss out.'

'Is someone coming with you?' Claire asked, noticing her client's disappointment.

'I really don't have anyone else. No family nearby and we've only just moved to Brisbane so I don't really know anybody yet.'

Claire could feel Lex's sense of isolation and sympathised with her. 'Ten o'clock, you say?' She consulted her appointment book. 'I'm free then—would you like some company?'

'Oh, yes, please!' Lex's sigh of relief was audible. 'I really didn't want to go by myself.'

'I'll meet you there at ten tomorrow.'

They watched her leave with a new spring in her step.

'That was a really nice thing to do.' Campbell's low voice intruded into Claire's thoughts.

He'd come closer again. There were only a few milli-metres separating them now. Appreciation sparked in his eyes. Nothing sexual. Just recognition of another person's kind heart.

He had the most expressive eyes Claire had ever seen. If he felt it or thought it, it was right there for the world to see. He'd obviously never had anything to hide. Claire envied him that.

'Nonsense,' she said, moving away. 'Anyone would have done the same thing.'

'No, Claire, they wouldn't.' His voice was serious.

'Goodbye, Campbell.'

Claire turned on her heel and left him standing in the corridor. He smiled at her dismissal but wasn't that easily perturbed. He followed her into the commonroom, catching up with her just as she had opened the fridge door and was rummaging around inside it. Her very appealing bottom was all he could see of her. He lounged in the doorway, allowing his male appreciation full rein. Soon enough she would dash it all with her shrewish tongue.

'Alone at last,' he said from the doorway.

Claire hit her head on a shelf and cursed under her breath. 'Do you mind?' she snapped. 'I thought you'd gone. You scared the living daylights out of me.' She rubbed her head.

'Sorry,' he said, trying to look suitably chastised.

Claire sat at the dining table, ignoring him. She opened her lunchbox as he pulled up a chair opposite.

'Why don't you date, Claire?'

So unexpected was his question that Claire nearly choked on the carrot stick she'd been eating. She coughed and spluttered and Campbell poured her a drink of water from the glass pitcher sitting in the middle of the table.

'Thank you,' she said in a raspy voice, taking a gulp of water. 'Is it so hard to believe that some women don't want to be in a relationship?'

'No, not at all.'

'Well, then, I guess I'm one of them.'

'There's a difference between not wanting to and choosing not to, Claire.'

'Oh, yeah? How?'

'Well, not wanting to indicates lack of interest. Choosing not to is a conscious decision that never allows for the possibility of something happening. It's choosing with your head.'

'Oh, I get it. You think I should choose with my heart.' Sarcasm laced her voice.

'I think you should *listen* to your heart. Don't just ignore it because you decided once upon a time that you weren't going to date.'

'And if I did listen to my heart? What makes you think it'd lead me to you?'

'Ah, that's easy.' He grinned a cheeky, schoolboy grin. 'I'm irresistible.'

'Oh, really.'

'Just ask my mum.'

'Oh, I'm sure to get an unbiased opinion there,' she said sarcastically.

'Hmm, you're right,' he mused thoughtfully, stealing a carrot stick from Claire's lunchbox. 'On second thoughts, ask my sisters. They have absolutely no illusions about me and they *still* think I'm irresistible.'

Campbell grinned again and stole a cherry tomato this time.

'Hey,' she protested feebly, growing weaker at the intimacy of him helping himself to her lunch.

'I'm starving,' he cajoled, and closed his eyes and sighed rapturously as he bit into the ripe, red flesh. 'Hmm. This tomato is delicious. So flavoursome.'

'My father grows them,' she said, distracted by his moan of enjoyment and the slow trickle of juice leaving the corner of his mouth.

Campbell opened his eyes and caught Claire staring. She was watching his chin where he could feel some juice trekking slowly downwards. Her stare was so intense and hungry he couldn't have been more surprised if she'd reached over and unzipped his fly. In fact, she might as well have, from the way his body was reacting.

'Claire, if you're trying to convince me that you don't want me, staring at me like that isn't the way to go about it.'

His words registered on a superficial level only. They didn't penetrate her intense concentration. She knew she shouldn't be looking but the juice drew her gaze like a moth to flame.

'Claire,' he whispered hoarsely.

It was a ragged, desperate sound that succeeded where his words hadn't. She gasped slightly, dragging her eyes away, shocked at her behaviour. It was practically X-rated. Her hand trembled as she passed him a paper napkin and tried to deny how bereft she felt that he was the one wiping the errant juice away and not her.

Oh, God, get a grip. What was the matter with her? Why did this man get to her so much?

'Is it because of him?'

'Him who?' she asked, wary again.

'The man you dated years ago who broke your heart. Or so the story goes.'

'Been snooping, Campbell?'

'No, not at all. It's amazing the stuff people will tell you.'

'Mind your own business,' she snapped, rising to wash her dishes at the sink.

'Oh, come on, Claire,' he persisted. 'If I'm paying the price for his sins, surely I deserve to know why.'

'Campbell!' She let her exasperation show.

'OK. I'll leave you be if you tell me.'

'Yeah, right.'

'I promise. Cross my heart.'

She turned to assess the honesty of his statement. He looked sincere and…it was way too good a deal to pass up. His relentless pursuit was annoying. Really, it was. And pointless. And as difficult as she found even breathing when he was near, she couldn't be with him. They had no future.

'All right.' Her shoulders sagged and she came back and sat at the table. 'We were young. No, correction, I was young. A third-year student nurse. Shane was a resident. We were in love, or at least…I was in love with him. He said he wanted to marry me and then some…stuff happened to do with my family and he…he dumped me.'

Campbell sat in silence as she laid out the bones of something that had obviously been such a big part of her life. Her complete lack of emotion as she gave just the facts spoke volumes about her hurt.

'How old were you?'

'Twenty.'

Campbell covered her hands with his. 'What stuff?'

'It doesn't matter now,' she said quietly, and removed her hands. She wasn't going to tell a virtual stranger things that even now were too painful to think about.

'Shane was a fool.' Campbell's voice held an edge of contempt.

She met his gaze and read the compassion in his emerald depths. Easy to say when he didn't know the half of it.

'No. It hurt for a long time but I think I'd have done the same thing if our situations had been reversed.'

It had been a traumatic chapter in her life. Her mother being diagnosed with Huntington's disease had been a gut-wrenching time. Not to mention the real possibility that the disease could have been inherited by herself. The last thing she had needed had been her fiancé deserting her in her hour of need. But he had.

It'd taken the better part of a year to get over Shane's betrayal. But with the passing of time, Claire had been able to see his side. It had been a tough call for someone in their prime, like Shane, to confront the possibility of his fiancée falling prey to a debilitating genetic illness. The hurt had dissipated but the determination not to make the same mistake with someone else lingered.

'I don't care what it was. If he'd really loved you, he'd have stayed.'

Claire shook her head sadly. Some things were too big, too awful to deal with. She knew that too well. 'You, Dr Deane,' she said, injecting a light teasing quality into her voice, 'are a romantic.'

'Guilty as charged,' he grinned. 'So, how about tonight?'

'Campbell! You promised.'

'Sorry, I lied. I had my fingers crossed behind my back.'

'You tricked me.' She glowered and marched back to the sink.

'You can't give up on men because of one stupid guy. I

won't let you. It's not fair to compare me to him. Give me a chance, I'll prove to you that we're not all the same.'

'Campbell,' she sighed, turning to face him, 'it's not just about Shane. There are other reasons…' Big reasons. 'He just helped to put everything into perspective.'

'I'm never going to give up, Claire. You may as well surrender now.'

'I've been pursued by some determined men, Campbell. I've never surrendered.'

'Honey, trust me. I bring new meaning to determined.'

'Well, bring it on, *honey*. But be prepared to lose.'

The instant her challenge was out Claire wished she could retract it. Damn him. Damn him for goading her into throwing down the gauntlet.

Campbell grinned. He felt an energy zinging through his body and revelled in how good and alive it made him feel. *She* made him feel. His pager beeped and he checked the message. 'Labour Ward. One of my ladies is in. I asked them to page me when she was ready to deliver.'

He walked slowly towards her as he talked, stopping a hand's length away. His gaze captured hers for a long moment.

'I'll be seeing you,' he said quietly, and walked away.

As it turned out, Claire reluctantly made her way to his office a few hours later with a document that required his signature urgently so she could send it off with the last courier run. Martin had been on the phone to her, harassing her about how important it was to have the document on the Minister's desk by close of business.

Internal mail would have been way too slow and the document too urgent and sensitive to trust to this not always reliable service.

Although Claire had resigned herself to doing the job

personally, she approached Campbell's office with a great deal of trepidation, the subtle challenge in his last words resonating in her head.

His door was closed and her hand shook as she knocked softly. Claire found herself wishing he'd left for the day, despite Martin's dire warnings, but his command to enter dashed the fantasy.

'Oh…sorry,' said Claire, taking in the two people sitting on the other side of Campbell's desk. 'I didn't realise you had clients…'

'Claire.' Campbell half stood, pleasure and surprise registering on his face. 'Come in.'

'No. It's OK. I'll come back.'

'No. Don't go. Stay. Actually, you've probably got some advice for Kay and Col.' He pulled up a chair next to the couple and she reluctantly sat down as he introduced her. 'Kay's pregnant with her second baby. They have a little boy who's three and has cystic fibrosis.'

Claire was pleased now for the seat. She couldn't believe what she was hearing. He wanted her to give advice on a genetic illness? He didn't know it, but he couldn't have picked a better person!

Claire's heart went out to the young couple. What terrible things they must have faced over the last three years, and now to have to confront the possibility of their new baby inheriting CF as well.

Every cell in her body rebelled at being part of this conversation. She wanted to get up and run. It was just way too close to home. She felt her heart beating painfully in her chest and was surprised they couldn't hear it in the room.

'Now…where were we?' He turned back to his clients. 'Oh, yes, the options. Well, you're only eight weeks so we can still investigate the baby's CF status with a special test called chorionic villi sampling. I can make an appointment for you right now,' he said, picking up the phone.

'Actually, no, Campbell, that won't be necessary,' said Col. 'We've talked about it and we've decided not to do that.'

'Ah…OK. Can I ask why?'

'We've had all the genetic counselling. We know we have a one in four chance of this baby inheriting CF, and we're OK with that. Obviously we don't wish it for our baby but if it happens, we'll deal with it.'

'Well, sure. It's your choice and you're obviously well informed, but a test at this early stage gives you options.'

'If we tested now and the baby was positive, we wouldn't be doing anything about it, so what's the point? We'll wait for the results of the heel prick after the baby's born, and in the meantime we'll be doing a lot of wishing and hoping and praying,' said Kay.

Claire admired her quiet resolve. It obviously wasn't easy for them. They were holding on tight to each other's hands as if one of them might fall if they let go.

Claire felt a pang and realised she envied their closeness. She gave herself a mental shake. This was crazy! When had this happened? Why would she feel jealous of this couple's relationship? It didn't make sense. But, then, a lot of things had changed since Campbell had entered her life— damn him!

Claire glanced across the desk at the man responsible for awakening feelings and emotions she doubted she'd ever felt before. She wanted to be angry with him but his obvious concern for this couple's plight softened her anger— double damn him!

While Claire understood totally where Kay and Col were coming from and empathised with their plight, she could tell Campbell didn't agree. He was being very professional.

Not pushing. Trying only to keep them as informed as possible. But Claire could read him like a book.

She knew how hard it was for some health professionals, particularly doctors, to take a step back sometimes. If there was a problem, they wanted to fix it or at least investigate it to the hilt in an attempt to fix it. They were healers. Doctors didn't like to sit back and not have the answers.

And then came the question she most dreaded.

'What do you think, Claire?' he asked earnestly, his green eyes begging her to support him.

She swallowed, her throat dry, trying to collect her thoughts on a subject she'd thought about every day for the last ten years.

'I think…' she started slowly, clearing her throat, 'I think…Kay and Col know better than anyone what's at stake, and they've obviously thought about it—a lot. You've done your bit, informing them of their choices, but ultimately the decision is theirs.'

'Campbell, we appreciate what you're trying to say. Really we do, but we've made up our mind.'

'All right, then.' Campbell smiled and stood and shook their hands. Claire stood also. 'It was great talking to you both and I'll see you again in four weeks. But, please, if you have any questions in the meantime, don't hesitate to contact me, OK?'

Claire watched Campbell as he showed his clients out, courteous and professional to the end. But Claire saw dissatisfaction in every line of his body. She knew what he was thinking, she had witnessed it often enough. He felt he had failed.

'Damn it,' he swore softly as he paced over to his window.

'You don't approve,' Claire said, not wanting to hear his

answer. Anything he said next she couldn't fail to take personally. It was too close to home.

'They don't need my approval Claire, I know that. It's just…' He raked his fingers through his glorious hair and turned to face her. 'I think they're going to go ahead and have a baby in the blind hope that it's not inflicted with an awful disease which, in reality, it has a very high chance of inheriting.'

'I don't think they're in denial over the risks, Campbell. I just think they're prepared to roll the dice and go with their lot.'

'What about the child? It's the one that's going to have to live with it.'

Despite understanding his sentiments, Claire could more than see the flip side. The fact that he couldn't irritated her.

'You think people with genetic illnesses can't live normal, fulfilled lives?'

'It's a debilitating lung disease,' he said, exasperation tinging his voice. 'I shouldn't have to tell you that. That child will spend the majority of its life either in hospital, taking meds or having physio and then dying too young.'

'If he or she has it.'

'If they take the test, they'll know. It'll buy them peace of mind.'

Having refused testing herself, Claire understood their reasons. How could knowing you or your child had a genetic disorder give you peace of mind?

'Ignorance can be bliss, Campbell,' said Claire, her voice stilted.

'I'm just saying…if it were me, I'd want to know. If it were me, I would think twice about bringing a child into the world if there was a history of genetic disease.'

And there it was. His statement hit her square in the solar

plexus. They were only words but they could sure wound. She almost staggered from their impact.

Claire knew what he meant, felt exactly the same way. Wasn't that why she had chosen to never have a baby herself? Why she'd even denied herself a relationship, so the temptation to conceive would never be an issue?

But, still, his statement stung. Any flutterings of attraction she may have felt for Campbell she needed to well and truly quash. If he knew the truth, he wouldn't want her. She couldn't bear to be rejected twice.

'But it's not you—is it?' Claire knew it wasn't a decision anyone else could make for you.

'No.' His admission was tinged with regret. He was silent for a moment. 'Anyway,' he said, shaking his head and pushing away from the window, 'You needed something?'

Claire admired his ability to change focus so quickly. She was having trouble processing their conversation. If she took nothing else away when she left the room, at least she knew where she really stood with him, even if he was completely oblivious to the fact.

'Claire?' he prompted, and she looked at him blankly. 'Wait? Maybe you didn't need anything? Maybe you've come to wave the white flag and go out to dinner with me?'

He laughed and she smiled despite the fog clogging her brain. He recovered easily after such a heavy conversation. He was too quick on his feet.

'Sorry, just a signature,' she said, handing him the document.

'Alas,' he mocked as he signed it and gave it back. 'I haven't forgotten your little challenge, Claire. In fact, I look forward to it.'

'You're wasting your time,' she stated, more calmly than she felt, turning on her heel and leaving the room.

She made her way back to the birth centre in a haze of

mixed emotions. Something was happening to her which she couldn't define. It was new and unwelcome and scary and all Campbell Deane's fault!

Before he'd come into her life she'd had clearly defined goals. Establish a birth centre. Make it strong and successful. Offer a real alternative to the women of Brisbane. Suddenly it didn't feel enough. She wanted more.

At least she now knew his views on genetic illness. He'd unwittingly given her the perfect weapon. All she had to do was tell him the truth and watch his interest die. See him run for the hills. Just like Shane.

But she knew she wouldn't. She'd made such a habit of concealing it she doubted she'd even know how to start. She didn't want people to treat her differently. She might have to live with it hanging over her head but she refused to let this disease define her.

It was her deep, dark, family secret. Her business and hers alone. And now, thankfully, a constant reminder to give Campbell Deane a wide berth.

CHAPTER THREE

WHEN Claire arrived at work the next morning a spectacular flower arrangement was waiting for her. 'Let the games begin,' she muttered to herself.

They were absolutely gorgeous. Claire knew they would have cost Campbell a fortune, with exotics like sprigs of wattle, grevillia, bird of paradise and dried rosellas. She fingered the card. Her impulse was to throw it in the bin but curiosity overwhelmed her. That they were from him was a foregone conclusion, but what words had he used to woo her? Romantic? Poetic? Flowery?

She glanced at the bold, black print. A gasp escaped involuntarily. Claire screwed it up and tossed it in her bin as if scalded.

LET THE GAMES BEGIN.

Was the man capable of reading her mind now? She didn't like it that he'd chosen the same words she'd only just thought. She didn't want to be on his wavelength.

Claire reeled in her frantic thoughts. It didn't matter. It wasn't going to happen. And if he thought that flowers would do it then he was sorely mistaken. Ignoring the part of her that loved, adored and appreciated things as beautiful as these flowers, she picked them up and marched them down to Obstetric Outpatients.

She dumped them in Andrea's arms, ignoring her surprise and curiosity. 'This place could do with some nice flowers to make it a little less hospital-like. Shove these in a few vases, will you?'

Andrea was well used to Claire's private life being a

50

taboo subject so she didn't ask. They had become firm friends over the years despite Claire's reticence over indulging too much personal information. Andrea knew that Shane had hurt her very badly, although Claire had never told her the reason for their break-up.

Before she could change her mind and snatch them back, Claire turned abruptly and left a stunned-looking Andrea in her wake. Mission accomplished, she sat down at her desk to review her day. Her concentration, however, was shot by the lingering scent of wattle.

'Who were the flowers from?' asked Pauline, entering the room and sitting at her desk. She was the centre's receptionist.

'Someone who hasn't got the message yet,' said Claire, her voice shorter and sharper than Pauline deserved.

'What did you do with them?'

'I gave them to Andrea down in Outpatients. It's too clinical-looking down there.'

'Claire,' Pauline said, with all the exasperated patience of someone who was well used to Claire's rejection of men. 'Next time, I'll have them. We could do with some around here, too.' Pauline laughed at Claire's unimpressed look. 'What poor man are you trying to annihilate with your rejection this time?'

'I wouldn't worry about this one. He's got pretty thick skin.'

'Pretty big wallet, too, judging by that bouquet.'

She was right. Claire was beginning to regret her rash action. She had been too hell-bent on getting them as far away from her as possible to think very rationally. All she knew was that she'd desperately wanted to bury her head in them and inhale their bushy fragrance. And if she'd succumbed to that temptation, she doubted she'd have been able to give them away.

And then they'd be sitting here on her desk, a constant reminder of him. He may as well be sitting on her desk because she knew that's all she'd be able to see when she looked at them. His smiling face, his red-blonde hair flopping in his eyes. Eyes that sparkled green and were so easy to read. His impressive physique…

She groaned and shook her head. No. She had done the right thing. Heaven knew, she was thinking about him enough now and the damn flowers were nowhere in sight. Despite her good intentions, too much of her time of late had been taken up by thoughts of Campbell. Her mind just kept wandering there of its own accord!

She made a determined effort to put him from her head and mentally braced herself for the day. She crossed her fingers and hoped that their paths wouldn't cross.

A very expensive bunch of flowers was an impressive opening salvo in this cat-and-mouse game they were playing. It was certainly going to be followed up. Claire braced herself for that also.

At ten o'clock Claire wandered into the radiology department and found Lex Craven sitting there, reading a magazine.

'How are you, Lex? Ready to see your baby?' Claire sat down beside her client.

'I'm so excited. I can't wait. I hope they're not running too late, I'm sure my bladder's going to burst any moment.'

Claire laughed. A full bladder was required for the scan. It provided a clearer picture of the uterus and the baby within it. Patients were told to drink at least a litre of water prior to their appointment. A big ask for many pregnant women.

Luck was on Lex's side when they were ushered in five minutes later. The radiologist, Darren, gave Lex a gown to change into.

'How's that baby of yours coming along, Darren? He must be six months old by now,' Claire asked. She had looked after Darren and his wife in Labour Ward and had delivered their son.

'Six months tomorrow. Impressive recall, Claire.'

Claire laughed. She did seem to have a photographic memory regarding the babies she had delivered. Claire was sure she could remember every baby she'd helped into the world. The moment of birth was so magical that each baby seemed to be indelibly imprinted into her memory bank. And if, occasionally, a birth did slip her mind, she only needed to refer to her scrapbook at home that had a picture and some basic information on all her deliveries. It was quite thick now, boasting over four hundred photos.

Lex rejoined them and climbed up onto the narrow bed. Darren pressed some buttons on the machine while Claire helped prepare Lex, exposing what was necessary and keeping everything else covered. Darren flicked a switch and killed the overhead lights.

'OK. Let's start. Goo first,' he said, squeezing a generous daub of the warmed gel onto Lex's tummy. A bright glow emitted from the screen and three pairs of eyes watched as the white static took form and shape as Darren applied the transducer and a twenty-week-old foetus filled the screen.

Claire took Lex's hand as she glimpsed tears shimmering in her client's eyes. Lex squeezed it gratefully and Claire didn't bother to let go.

'OK, I'm just going to check the placenta first,' he informed Lex, running the transducer around until he found what he was looking for. 'Good position,' he murmured. 'Now, we start from the head and work down. I'll be taking various measurements as I go.'

Darren explained what he was looking at as he went methodically from head to toe. He looked at the brain and took some measurements, satisfying himself that it was the right size. He checked other brain structures and calculated the diameter of the baby's skull.

Next he looked at the face, paying particular attention to the mouth and lips, checking for any abnormality. It was a perfect face. Two eyes, two ears, one nose. He moved down further and found two lungs and then visualised the tiny, beating heart. Satisfied there were four chambers and all associated structures were present, he pressed a button and the room filled with the noise of the baby's strong, regular heartbeat.

'There's the baby's stomach,' Darren informed them, as he moved lower.

'Yeah right. I'll have to take your word for that,' said Lex with a laugh.

Claire knew exactly how she felt. Ultrasound was a specialised field and what was obviously a stomach to Darren looked like a blob of black and white fuzzy nothing to most other people. He found the liver and kidneys as well. The spinal column was thoroughly checked to make sure it was complete.

'All intact,' Darren murmured, as much to himself as to Claire and Lex.

The baby was active during the procedure, allowing them a good view of everything. Ten fingers and toes were all accounted for.

'Do you want to know the sex?' Darren asked.

'Can you tell?'

'Uh-huh.'

Lex looked at Claire questioningly. Claire shrugged noncommittally.

'I didn't want to. We discussed it and we wanted it to be a surprise. But…oh, gosh, I can't believe how tempted I am.'

'Yeah, I know what you mean,' said Darren. 'We were tempted, too.'

'No. Don't tell me. Brian will kill me if I found out.'

Darren took some measurements of the baby's thighbone next. He entered the data into his machine. With all the other measurements he'd imput, it would now calculate the growth of the baby, its weight and its precise gestation.

Claire felt tears prick her eyes at the wonder of this developing life, still only half-developed in medical terms but already a fully formed little person being nurtured and protected in the safety of the womb. She felt an ache deep inside, an emptiness that she had suppressed for years, refusing suddenly to be quelled. Watching Lex's baby on the screen, Claire felt a yearning begin and then intensify.

What was the matter with her? Babies had been part of her working life for over a decade. When had they started to get to her like this? At twenty, after her mother's diagnosis, Claire knew she would never allow herself to bring a baby of her own into this world. It had been difficult to come to terms with, but she'd felt she hadn't really had a choice.

Maybe she hadn't taken the appropriate time to grieve? For someone who loved babies as desperately as Claire did, never achieving motherhood was a real loss. Losses needed to be mourned. She should have cried, but she hadn't. She should have railed against the fates, but she hadn't done that either. She'd felt immensely sad but had moved on with her life. Forged a career.

Was she doing it now? Grieving? Was that what was happening to her? And why now? What had happened to trigger it? And then Campbell poked his head in the door and something deep inside her knew it was him. He was responsible for this discontent. She shut her mind to it. She didn't want to go there.

'Here you all are,' he said cheerfully, closing the door behind him, along with the bright outside lights that intruded into the darkened room.

'Campbell,' said Lex, delight in her voice. 'Come and look at my beautiful baby.'

Campbell did as he'd been bidden and admired the ultrasound images, oblivious to Claire's turmoil.

'Beautiful. Absolutely, no doubt.'

Claire raised her head to discover him staring at her. His look immobilised her. Even breathing was difficult when he looked at her with such hunger. Claire blinked rapidly to dispel the moisture that had dewed her eyes. It was too late. He'd seen it. She could see his eyes narrow with concern. Even in the gloom he was very easy to read.

'Looks like you're spot on, Lex,' Darren continued. He was so focused, Claire doubted he'd even registered Campbell's presence. Pity she couldn't say the same for herself. 'Twenty weeks and one day, according to the calculations.'

With the scan over, Darren flicked the lights on and Claire helped Lex down from the narrow bed. She rushed off gratefully to relieve her full bladder. Darren left the room to retrieve the video recording for Lex. Campbell, his back to the wall, watched Claire.

'Clinic smells nice today,' he commented casually. 'Wattle, I believe.'

'Yes, I thought it could do with a few humanising touches.'

He laughed and she ignored him.

'Where will you send tomorrow's flowers?' he asked, amusement in his voice.

'I was hoping you'd get the message today.'

He looked at her with a bemused expression. There

would be flowers tomorrow. And the next day and the day after that…until she surrendered.

'Pauline, our receptionist, has first dibs.'

He laughed harder and Claire was drawn to the way his hair flopped forward, almost in his eyes. He looked so little-boy endearing, she had to quell an urge to ruffle it. He wasn't a boy and this wasn't child's play.

'You can send me flowers from here to Christmas, Campbell, I won't be changing my mind.'

'I thought women liked receiving gifts?'

'Well, I guess that depends on the motive of the sender.'

Lex re-entered the room, out of her gown and looking more like herself.

'Darren's going to leave the recording at the desk,' Claire said.

'Oh, fantastic. Brian was so disappointed he couldn't be here. He's going to be rapt when he sees it. I just hope I remember everything.'

'You'll be fine,' said Claire, waving goodbye. 'See you in a few weeks. Take care. Ring if you have any problems.'

'You know,' Campbell said after the door had closed behind Lex, 'when I first arrived, I could have sworn you looked like you were about to burst into tears. For an awful moment, I thought something must have been wrong with the baby.'

Claire remained silent.

'You looked so…stricken.'

'I did not look stricken,' she snapped. Had she looked that bad? Had it been that obvious?

'Whatever.' He shrugged. 'I mean, I was pleased just to be able to read any sort of emotion in your face.'

'Oh, so I'm cold now?' she asked waspishly.

'No. You're just…guarded. What made you that way, Sister West?'

'Life.'

'Why haven't you got a couple of babies of your own?'

Campbell's question caught her completely off guard. It hit her like a sledgehammer to the heart. She gasped and stared at him, dumbstruck. Had he seen that much? Could he have guessed the cause of her tears?

'Maybe I don't want any.' Her heart pounded loudly, each beat mocking her. Liar. Liar. Liar.

'I don't believe that. C'mon, Claire, you've immersed yourself in babies for years. You don't do that if you're indifferent.'

'Exactly.' She forced a light note into her voice. 'I've witnessed labour first-hand many times. I've seen how much it hurts. I'm not silly.' She smiled a fake smile but Campbell was clearly unconvinced. 'Just because I'm a midwife, that doesn't mean I'd be a good mother.'

'I don't believe that either.'

'Since when is this any of your business, anyway? How would you like it if I asked you such prying questions?'

'Shoot.'

Claire glared at him. Typical. Trust him to call her bluff. Stubborn, exasperating man. 'Fine. Why haven't you had children, Campbell? Or don't you want them either?'

'I can't wait to have kids,' he said and grinned. 'I think I'd be a fantastic dad.'

Claire had to agree with him there. He would make a great dad. She should have known he'd want children. But he wouldn't want her children. Her children with her mutant genes.

'So what are you waiting for?' she asked, trying to keep a bitter edge from her voice.

'Haven't found the right woman yet. Well...' He winked. 'Until now.'

'Argh! Campbell!' She stalked to the door and yanked it

open. The conversation in here was getting too uncomfortable.

'I told you I was obstinate.' Claire caught his words just
as the door closed behind her and shut him out of her sight.

Obstinate was a good word, Claire acknowledged after two
weeks of floral gifts. Every morning a bunch of flowers,
each more exquisite than the last, greeted her. Gorgeous,
expensive creations that were increasingly difficult to give
away. She did, however, part with every single bloom.

The hospital grapevine was working overtime as Claire
went from ward to ward, spreading her floral cheer.
Somehow they'd discovered the identity of the man responsible so Claire couldn't even pretend she didn't know
him.

'Give in, Claire,' said Andrea from the clinic, as Claire
passed her with yet another bouquet.

'Andrea, how long have we known each other?'

'Eleven years.'

'So you know I don't date.' Exasperation tinged her
voice.

'Claire, it's been a long time. I know Shane hurt you but
surely you're over him by now.'

'Of course I am.' Claire sighed heavily, weary of having
to explain her motives. 'But that's the thing—doesn't he
remind you of Shane? I mean, if I was going to suddenly
start dating again, why would I choose someone who's exactly like my ex?'

'Are you crazy? He's nothing like Shane.'

'They both have red hair and a reputation.'

'And that's where the similarities end. My God, you
can't be serious! Shane's reputation was justified. He was
superficial, conceited and arrogant. He flirted with every-

one, including me. He was a creep! And he wasn't even a very good doctor.'

Claire listened to her friend in silence. 'Why have you never told me any of this?'

'You loved him, Claire. He could do no wrong. What would I have gained from that except maybe a ruined friendship?'

Claire absently sniffed the bouquet in her arms while she digested Andrea's words.

'Look, I've worked with Campbell a lot in Outpatients. I can tell you he has more integrity in his little finger than Shane had in his entire body. And he's a fantastic obstetrician. Don't judge him by Shane's standards. Do yourself a favour...cut him a break.'

'No point,' Claire said, straightening her back and hardening her heart, ignoring the truth in Andrea's words. 'I don't date. No exceptions.'

Andrea's words gave Claire food for thought as she went on her way. Maybe comparing Campbell and Shane had been doing Campbell a disservice. So they both had red hair—a minor superficial physical resemblance. Apart from that, they really were nothing alike.

Claire had to admit Andrea's description of Shane's character was more than accurate and despite keeping her distance from him, Claire knew enough about Campbell to know that his red hair was where his likeness with Shane ended. And he was definitely, no contest, a much better doctor.

But, Claire reminded herself sharply, whether he looked like her ex-fiancé or not was immaterial. There were other reasons to keep her distance. Much more serious ones. The fact that his appearance had stirred up some long forgotten wounds helped make it all the easier to stay away.

If only the rest of the hospital staff would make it just

as easy. Instead, Campbell was fast gaining notoriety throughout St Jude's as the underdog. Claire had become the tyrant! Poor brave Campbell pitted against Big Bad Claire who rebuffed him heartlessly, rejecting his expensive romantic gestures. She'd even heard that one ward was running a sweep on who would win the battle.

Claire detested being the subject of gossip. Heaven knew, she'd spent most of her working life at St Jude's being a curiosity. Who? Claire West? Oh, the one who doesn't date? I hear she's a lesbian. And on and on. Nonetheless, every bunch of flowers hardened her resolve. Let them talk. A relationship with Campbell was out of the question.

Campbell was conspicuous by his absence. But she knew his game. His strategy was to keep a low profile and let his gifts work their magic. He was hoping she'd be so overwhelmed and flattered she'd be begging for a date. Well, she was on to him and it wasn't going to work.

However, when flowers arrived on the Friday of the second week, Claire knew she had to protest. She dialled his room number, knowing he did a clinic at this time.

'Campbell Deane.' His voice was warm and sexy, and Claire gripped the receiver as her heart tripped. How could a voice affect her in such a way?

'Stop it, Campbell. No more flowers.'

'Ready to surrender?'

She could hear the humour in his voice and knew his green eyes would be twinkling. 'No. I've just had enough. I'm running out of vases.'

'That's not what I hear. The rest of the hospital has a vase shortage. In fact, you seem to be the only one with available vases. Maybe you could loan them some of yours.'

'They go in the bin come Monday. Enough.'

'You want me to stop sending flowers?'

'Good. You're catching on.'

'Come and ask me. Face to face.'

'What?' He had to be joking!

'I'll be in my consulting room for another fifteen minutes.'

Claire gawped at the dead phone. He'd hung up! Why, of all the… So he wanted an audience, huh? She rose to her feet. She'd make him sorry he was so damned imperious!

Anger carried her to his office before she realised she'd just done exactly what he wanted. She stormed in without knocking and found him leaning against his desk, facing the door. Waiting for her.

'Six minutes.' He whistled as his gaze fell to the rapid rise and fall of her chest and the way the fabric of her uniform pulled across her breasts. 'I see you took the stairs.'

'It was faster,' she snapped.

'Before you start…' he held up his hands to placate her '…I apologise.' He pushed himself off the desk and walked slowly towards her. As he advanced a step she retreated a step. 'I just wanted to see your face again and I figured…well, if you were steamed up enough…'

Claire bumped against the wall. Campbell halted also. An arm's length separated them. His apology had taken the wind out of her sails.

'I'd forgotten how beautiful you are, Claire. Staying away has been so hard but I thought, well, you know, absence is supposed to make the heart grow fonder.' He stepped closer.

'Campbell.' Desperation tinged her voice. 'Stop this, please.' She pressed her hands against his chest to prevent him from coming any closer.

'You don't want me to send you any more flowers?'

Claire nodded, not quite trusting her voice, which she felt sure would betray her trembling. With Campbell so close, her entire body was quivering. She'd forgotten how magnificent he was in the flesh. I can't let this happen. I can't.

'I thought women loved flowers,' he said quietly, staring at her mouth as his head inched closer.

'I...I hate them.' Her voice tripped over the lie.

'Really?' he whispered.

'I do now,' she whispered back, swallowing to moisten her suddenly parched throat. I can't let this happen.

The room was silent. All that could be heard was the ticking of the wall clock and the thunder of two galloping heartbeats.

'Kiss me. Kiss me and I'll stop.'

She felt his warm breath on her face as he uttered the outrageous request. Only it didn't seem so outrageous now. In fact, to Claire's ears it seemed like a very sensible suggestion. His lips were so close, she was mesmerised. She couldn't think of one reason why she shouldn't. And she wanted to. Lordy, she wanted to.

He placed his arms against the wall on either side of her head. Her hands were being crushed by his body weight—a completely ineffective barrier—as he inched closer. And suddenly she could bear the suspense no longer. She closed the millimetres that separated their lips and surrendered to the decadence of the moment.

It had been a long time since she'd kissed a man. She expected Campbell to lead and dominate, and he didn't disappoint. He devoured her mouth, plundering its softness, branding hers lips with his own. It wasn't hard or savage, just thorough. It was like this kiss was his sales pitch and he was giving her all he had.

It went on and on, sucking her every breath from her body, shattering the memory of any kiss she'd ever had before this one. They were nothing compared to this. It was blinding and drugging and left her wanting more.

She clung to him, revelling in her sweet surrender. The lyrics of an old country song came to her mind. 'I feel sorry for any one who isn't me tonight.' She'd reached nirvana.

He pulled back and she gasped in a ragged breath. They stilled and he rested his forehead against hers as their breathing settled.

'Claire…?' he murmured in a throaty whisper.

And it brought her crashing back to the real world. She straightened up and he dropped his arms, allowing her some space to move away. She crossed to the window, completely oblivious to the million-dollar view of Brisbane's skyscrapers.

I can't let this happen. I can't. The frantic beating of her heart refused to settle and Claire knew it needed a prod.

'So.' She cleared her throat. Even to her own ears she sounded like a woman who'd just been kissed—breathy and husky. She turned to face him. 'No more flowers, right?'

'You used me,' he accused, laughter in his voice.

Yeah, right. He looked like someone who'd been used and abused, completely against his will. More like the cat that had swallowed the bloody canary.

'You practically sexually harassed me. You deserved it.'

'Good point,' he said, straightening his tie. 'No more flowers. I promise.'

He looked so appealing, standing there all rumpled and obviously affected by their kiss. She had to get out of there before she threw him on his desk and he *could* accuse her of sexual harassment. It had been a long time.

'As if that's worth the paper it's written on,' she quipped, walking past him with her head held high. She didn't look back, just walked straight out of his door and closed it firmly.

Claire spent the weekend in a flurry of activity. The entire house, inside and out, was cleaned. The garden was weeded. Her car was washed. Idle time was her enemy.

The minute she stopped doing something memories of Friday and the kiss would crowd in and then other thoughts and feelings that she couldn't afford to nurture came along, too. She needed to work. She had to work! Anything to stop herself from thinking.

She mustn't entertain fanciful thoughts. Just because he had kissed her like she'd never been kissed before, it was no reason to go and lose her head. There were too many reasons why it wouldn't work.

She fell into bed each night exhausted, hoping for the kind of sleep that was deep and dreamless. But even in sleep he occupied space in her head and she woke each morning tired and cranky and confused. Damn him!

On Monday, a box of sinfully rich chocolate truffles, beautifully gift-wrapped, was waiting for her. Great. Her biggest weakness next to flowers and men with red hair. She groaned and opened the card.

NO FLOWERS. A PROMISE IS A PROMISE.

Campbell was again conspicuous by his absence as each day a box of chocolates arrived. She gave them away, too, but did allow herself the odd indulgence from each box. She wasn't weakening, she was just being practical. A person had to eat.

A week passed and Campbell hadn't contacted her. The weekend came and went and Monday morning saw another delivery of chocolates, more heavenly than the last five. Claire knew she should ring him and demand that he stop, but with their kiss and its emotional fallout still fresh in her mind she didn't think she was up to another audience with Campbell.

She knew it was the reason for his silence. He was biding his time until she tired again of his persistence and initiated contact. This time she wasn't going to give him another opportunity to steal a kiss.

Claire put the fact that she'd actually kissed him to one side. He'd probably had it planned all along. The minute she'd walked into his office…probably even before that. She'd bet he'd been plotting how to get a kiss from her.

And despite all the reasons she shouldn't, Claire doubted she could be strong enough to resist a second taste of his lips. Never in all her experience of men had she ever met the like of Campbell. Rationally she knew that starting something wasn't possible or even fair, but she was struggling with an inner resistance that seemed to have sprung from nowhere.

Claire opened the box and absently chose a chocolate, her mind reliving the kiss for the hundredth time. Her phone rang and she was grateful for its intrusion. She'd spent far too much time daydreaming about Campbell lately.

Campbell was smiling as he shut the door. What a great way to end the week and put you in a good mood—delivering a baby. And what a whopper! Four and a half kilos! No wonder the mother, who had endured a long and exhausting labour, had required some suturing. As Campbell strode past the nurses' station the sweet aroma of chocolate wafted out to meet him. His stomach grumbled and he realised it was lunchtime.

He chose a chocolate and popped it into his mouth. He knew they were the ones he'd ordered for Claire this morning. He'd specifically asked for a box of heart-shaped chocolates. Her continual rebuffing was beginning to irk. Especially when he saw his gifts being enjoyed by the entire St Jude's nursing staff. Especially when he couldn't sleep at night from thinking about that kiss.

'Great chocolates, Campbell. Thanks,' said one of the labour ward nurses with a cheeky grin as she chose one and scurried off.

Campbell straightened his tie, took another chocolate and decided it was now or never. He wondered if Claire liked chocolate-flavoured kisses. He had to have more of her sweet lips.

He found her at her desk, writing industriously in a chart. She hadn't heard him so he lounged against the doorframe for a while. The heavy swing of her raven hair obscured her face, so on she wrote, completely oblivious to his presence. He liked being near her. Even with an office and several desks' distance between them, he could feel his body's cells responding. It was hard for him to describe what it was, the feeling was so basic, so elemental. But he liked it.

'You look like you could do with some lunch, Sister West.' He watched as her pen stilled and she slowly peeked out from behind the curtain of her hair. 'Hello, Claire. How are you?'

'Four kilos heavier, thanks to you. Lunch is out—I'm on a diet.'

'So...' he laughed '...you didn't give them all away?'

'I sampled a few,' she said, and turned back to her notes.

Claire allowed her hair to swing forward again. Seeing him so unexpectedly had brought him squarely back into her focus. And in the last few days she'd been doing so well, relegating him to the far reaches of her grey matter. Only her dreams visited him there.

'Lunch, Claire?' Her dismissal amused him.

'Can't do,' she said, not bothering to look away from her notes. 'I'm expecting Shirley Miller any moment.'

'The breech?'

Claire heard the doors to the unit open. 'Perfect timing.' She looked up and grinned. She was careful not to come into contact with Campbell's lounging body as she passed him to greet Shirley. Even just walking nearby, her body responded. It trembled as if they were two magnets, irresistibly drawn to each other.

All thoughts of Campbell fled when Shirley doubled over and clutched her husband's arm.

'What's up, Shirley?' asked Claire, remaining calm. She guided her client into one of the birthing suites, motioning to Campbell to stay where he was.

'I don't know,' she said, straightening. 'I've been having a lot of false labour pains over the past couple of days and some nagging backache. But just now, in the car park, I think I had a couple of contractions.'

'OK,' said Claire. 'Are you all right to lie down while I feel the baby's position?'

'It's still breech. It hasn't turned,' said Shirley as her husband helped her onto the bed.

Claire gently palpated her client's very pregnant abdomen. 'Hmm. You're right. You're, what…thirty-seven weeks now?'

'Yes.'

Claire paused, removing her hands as Shirley had another contraction. She gripped Claire's hand hard as Claire watched the clock to time the contraction. Ninety seconds.

'They're bad, aren't they?'

'Yes.' Shirley grimaced.

'Right. Well, I think we need to get you up to Labour

Ward straight away. I'm sorry but, as I already explained, we can't do a breech birth here.'

'I know. It's all right. Frankly, I just want this baby out. I don't care how or where you do it.'

'OK,' Claire laughed. 'We can do an internal when we get there.' Claire popped her head out the door.

'What's happening?' Campbell asked.

'Still breech but definitely in labour. Grab the wheelchair from the storeroom, will you? You can accompany us up to Labour Ward.'

'Oh, so I do have my uses,' he teased.

'Just get the wheelchair.'

Campbell did as he was asked and entered the room shortly afterwards, pushing the chair just as Claire was helping Shirley off the bed. 'Your chariot, madam,' he said with a flourish, and bowed.

Shirley and her husband laughed. As she turned to sit in the chair, she cried out and her membranes ruptured. Amniotic fluid flooded over the chair and floor.

'Oh, God. I'm sorry,' Shirley apologised.

'It's fine, don't worry,' Claire assured her, grabbing some hospital-issue towels and throwing them onto the puddle on the floor.

Shirley clutched her stomach and her eyes grew wide in alarm.

'What?' asked Campbell.

'It's coming. The baby's coming now!'

Campbell and Claire exchanged the briefest look and sprang into action. They knew that a woman who had been through this three times already could give birth quickly. They also knew that often, when a mother made such an alarming statement, she was spot on.

'Right, Shirley,' said Campbell, his voice calm and confident. 'We're going to need to have a look at what's happening. I know this may be difficult right now, but the most important thing to remember is not to push. OK? You can pant but don't push. Are you comfortable standing? It really is the best position to deliver the baby. It's better to have gravity on our side.'

'This is fine,' Shirley agreed.

'If your husband…?'

'Graham,' Claire supplied.

'Graham could support under your arms and you lean back into him… That's great,' he complimented them as Graham supported his wife perfectly.

Campbell pushed the wheelchair out of the way and got down on his hands and knees on the towels. Claire followed suit.

Shirley was absolutely right. The baby *was* coming. In fact, as Claire removed Shirley's underthings it was evident that it was already there. Adrenaline accelerated her heartbeat as they looked at the baby's bottom and scrotum bulging from the birth canal.

'Delivered any breeches before?' Campbell asked quietly.

'A few, when I worked out west. You?'

'I studied for six months under a French obstetrician who specialised in breech deliveries. I delivered plenty while I was there. So we can do this, OK? Remember the cardinal rule? Hands off the breech.'

'Let's do it.' She smiled and he squeezed her hand.

His confidence buoyed her. The potential for complications increased with a breech presentation. It was good to have an experienced obstetrician by her side.

Claire got up and pulled a trolley close. Campbell grabbed some gloves and pulled them on.

'OK, Shirley, your little boy is going to be here soon.'

'B-boy?'

'Yes, the evidence is hanging free for all to see. I'm just going to have a feel and see where the legs are, OK?'

'Sure,' she panted.

Campbell inserted two fingers and shut his eyes, concentration puckering his brow. 'It's a frank,' he said, removing his hand. A breech in a frank position meant that the legs were jackknifed onto the abdomen—the commonest form of breech.

'You're doing so well, Shirley. At the next contraction, feel free to push with it, OK? We'll see if the legs will come out without any help.'

'Oh, boy, another one—now,' she said, starting to breathe heavily.

'Go with it, Shirley. Big push for me.'

Shirley bellowed loudly as she bore down. The legs slipped out in textbook style and the baby was now visible up to his belly button.

'This baby sure wants out, Shirley,' Campbell joked. 'He's doing all the right things. He's practically delivering himself.'

Campbell pulled a loop of umbilical cord down to give them some slack for when the rest of the body made its appearance. The baby started cycling his legs, slowly inching himself out, obviously determined to be born. The arms and shoulders came out next. The baby was almost completely out now. Only the head remained.

'Wonderful, Shirley,' Claire soothed. 'You're doing really well. The head will be out soon.'

'I'll hold you to that.' A flushed and sweaty-faced Shirley attempted humour.

Campbell was supporting the baby's weight, cupping his bottom. His other hand spanned the tiny chest to slow the delivery while they waited for the next contraction to deliver the head.

Both Claire and Campbell knew that delivering the head was the crucial time and the one most fraught with potential complications. With a normal delivery the head was the first part out, having fully dilated the cervix and vaginal opening to accommodate it. With a breech, the head was the last part to come out, so if full dilatation hadn't occurred, and particularly if the head was large, the baby could get stuck.

Shirley moaned as another pain contracted her uterus. Graham comforted and encouraged her as he took her weight. Campbell continued to support the baby as the back of the head cleared the birth canal. They could see the nape of the neck now. Shirley cried out as her birth outlet slowly stretched to allow the passage of her baby's head.

Campbell supported the baby as it slipped out. He stood and placed the newborn in his mother's arms. Jubilation reigned supreme as the baby wailed lustily. Claire felt hot tears prick her eyes. She let them shine, not caring whether Campbell saw them or not. What a rush! The birth centre's first birth, and a breech! Shirley and Graham stood in the middle of the room, hugging and laughing and crying.

Putting her excitement aside, Claire covered the wet newborn in a warmed blanket and helped Shirley to the bed. The job wasn't finished yet. The cord had stopped pulsing so she clamped it and showed Graham how to cut it. She administered an intramuscular injection of a drug that stimulated uterine contraction, and then she delivered the placenta.

Frivolity, excitement and laughter ebbed and flowed around her as Claire completed her responsibilities. Campbell sat on the bed with the new parents, admiring the latest addition to their family. Claire watched him surreptitiously. It was good to see the grin couldn't be wiped from his face either. It made her own smile even bigger.

A quiet knock at the door interrupted the celebrations. It was Valerie Baines. She was one of the centre's midwives who'd come in especially today to attend a training course. She'd been out to lunch.

'Oh! I leave you alone for an hour and you deliver our very first baby!' she exclaimed.

'A breech, too,' said Claire.

'Such clever people,' she teased, and joined in the excited gathering, cooing at the baby and congratulating everyone.

'This requires a celebration,' Valerie declared half an hour later after the paperwork had been completed and the room put to rights. 'Let's crack open that bottle of champagne we've been keeping for this occasion.' She ran off to get it.

She returned with the chilled bottle and five glasses. They clinked them together and toasted the baby—David John Miller. The newborn slept peacefully in his father's arms. He'd had a tough day, too. They also toasted Claire and Campbell and the birth centre.

'To you.' Campbell raised his glass to Claire as Valerie helped Shirley to the shower, husband in tow.

Claire stroked her finger down the soft red cheek of baby David. 'Ditto.' She smiled and they grinned at each other like idiots. Claire felt the attraction between them treble. She was in real trouble! 'You know Martin is going to have a fit over this, don't you?'

'Let him,' he said and laughed. They toasted that as well.

Claire had to admit that working beside Campbell had been exhilarating. She'd seen another side to the man who had pursued her so persistently. The dedicated doctor. Cool and calm in a situation that would have tested most doctors' mettle. And he wasn't afraid to get on his haunches to deliver a baby. She felt her admiration for him rise and mix with her burgeoning attraction. The champagne must have gone to her head.

Campbell stared at the very different Claire in front of him. Her cheeks glowed and her brown eyes were as tempting as the expensive chocolates he'd been sending her. For once he could read everything in their sweet depths. She wanted him. It was there, as plain as day. He should have plied her with champagne a month ago.

'Have dinner with me tonight.' He held his breath.

'OK.' She grinned. Yup. It had definitely gone to her head.

CHAPTER FOUR

CLAIRE sat beside the bed, holding her mother's bony, frail hand. Her thumb stroked rhythmically over the papery skin. Right here in front of her lay the reason that a relationship with any man was impossible.

The clock in the lounge room chimed seven, breaking into her reverie. Time to go. She leaned forward and gently kissed her mother's cheek. Mary didn't stir.

'I'd better go, Dad,' she said, locating her father in his bedroom, watching the evening news.

'Goodnight, darling.' He smiled his gentle smile. 'Claire…'

'Yes?'

'I don't mean to interfere…but…you know you don't have to come home tonight. I can manage just fine.'

'Dad,' she joked in mock horror. 'You're not suggesting I spend the night with this man on the first date?'

He smiled, a rare occasion of late. 'Seriously, darling, it's been years since you've been on a date. I want you to enjoy yourself for a change.'

'I have to be here in the morning, Dad. She expects me.'

'She's not your responsibility, Claire.'

'Dad…she's my mother.'

'You're young, you're supposed to be selfish and irresponsible. I can manage.'

'I know but…she'll fret if I'm not here.'

'Darling, she probably won't even be aware.' His voice cracked and Claire had to swallow hard.

'She'll know,' Claire insisted. She walked into the room

and kissed him on the head. 'I've got my mobile. Call me if you need to. I mean it, Dad. Anything. See you in the morning.'

Claire pulled out of her driveway, her mind preoccupied with her mother's illness and her father's devotion. He deserves a medal, she thought as she pulled up at the lights. She chewed absently at the inside of her lip, worrying about the future.

She gave herself a mental shake as the car behind her hooted to let her know that the light had turned green. Her thoughts should be on the evening ahead and Campbell. If she was going to worry about anything tonight, it should be him.

He'd wanted to come and pick her up but she had insisted on going to the restaurant independently.

'Is that so you can make a fast getaway?' he had asked.

'Huh! My plan is foiled,' she had quipped, and he had laughed and left it alone.

Not for the first time, she admonished herself for her rash acceptance of his invitation. Once the euphoria from little David's birth had ebbed, her doubts had resurfaced. She'd even attempted to page him and cancel, but he must have already left for the day.

If she had known his home phone number she would have tried him there. But she didn't, so here she was, feeling rather like she was driving to her doom instead of a pleasant evening with a nice man.

Her gaze fell on her mobile phone and she pushed aside the temptation to ring the restaurant and cancel through a third party, like a coward. She also quelled the urge to just drive around for a few hours and then go home.

Stand him up? After he'd hunkered down on his hands and knees in a pool of amniotic fluid and helped her deliver a baby? And not just any baby, but one that a lot of obstetricians would have baulked at delivering. That seemed pretty churlish.

So. She'd go. As a thank you and nothing else. She'd be polite and companionable and beat a hasty retreat as soon as was possible. Easy. Simple.

And if her thoughts turned fanciful, all she need do was picture her mother. Remember her just as she had left her this evening, lying in bed, ravaged by a cruel disease, waiting to die. That should do it.

Claire arrived at the restaurant only a little late. She hadn't really known what to expect. She'd assumed it would be something posh and à la carte. So to find a small Italian joint off the beaten track was a pleasant surprise.

Claire had been unsure what to wear so had decided on a very plain sleeveless linen shift dress with a modest neckline and an even more modest hemline, falling below the knee. She had chosen it because of its simplicity. She hadn't wanted to wear anything too provocative and give Campbell the wrong idea.

If she'd known that the moment she'd slipped it over her head the dress went from simple to sexy, she'd never have worn it. It was the colour. A bright fire-engine red, which complemented her olive skin and accentuated the richness of her black hair. The colour naturally drew attention but, once gained, the vision of her in it was one not easy to forget.

Well, she sure knew how to make an entrance, Campbell thought as two waiters nearly collided in their haste to seat her. She did look ravishing, and Campbell understood the effect she was having on them. But the most important thing was that she was here with him, finally. The wait had been worth it.

A young Latin-looking waiter, the apparent victor between the two, ushered her to the table where Campbell waited. He half rose politely as the waiter pulled her chair out and then spread a starched linen napkin on her lap, lingering a little longer than Campbell felt was appropriate. Victor or not, Campbell was going to break his fingers if he touched Claire again. Anywhere. At all.

Claire could feel Campbell's scrutiny as the waiter fussed and took her drink order. She was pleased to be sitting because Campbell in casual mode was a sight to behold. Having seen him in nothing but suits and ties, it was an unexpected pleasure to find him in faded denim jeans and an open-necked polo shirt, which clung to the firm muscles of his arms and chest.

They regarded each other steadily over a wax-encrusted Chianti bottle complete with flickering candle. Damn! The lingering memory of his devastating kiss swamped her traitorously. Claire could feel her resolve weakening and the internal struggle she had fought with herself from the minute she'd met him seemed less important by candlelight.

'I thought you were going to stand me up,' he said, the candlelight accentuating the blond highlights in his hair.

'So did I.' She smiled and he laughed.

'I'm pleased you didn't.' He raised his water glass. She raised hers and they clinked them together.

'This place is nice. Kind of quaint. Authentic.'

'It's my favourite place to eat out. You can keep all those fancy places with their nouvelle cuisine. Me, I like good hearty food and lots of it. Places that serve you up a teaspoon of food in the middle of a huge plate just don't do it for me. I hope you're not disappointed.'

'On the contrary.' She shrugged her slim shoulders, her bob brushing against them. 'I agree. I can't bear the pretentiousness of those places.'

'So you're not one of these women who just nibble when they go on dates?'

'Absolutely not. If you think I'm going to sit here and pick at a garden salad all night, think again. I'm in the mood for lasagne.'

'Your choice in cuisine is matched only by your choice in clothes,' he complimented her. 'You look amazing tonight. That dress and the candlelight...wow!'

Claire blushed and laughed. Their gazes held and locked. The heat between them could have lit a thousand candles.

The waiter arrived to take their order and Claire released her breath. Campbell ordered lasagne for her and marinara for himself. He also ordered a bottle of red wine, which arrived promptly.

'To the birth centre.' He raised his glass.

'To breech births,' she countered.

'To little Davy,' he agreed, and clinked his glass against hers.

'Thank you for today, Campbell. Your ability and professionalism impressed me. You said you studied in France for a while?'

'Yes. There's an obstetrician there, Henri Busson, he's quite well known.'

'Yes, I've read some of his papers.'

'He has his own private clinic. Women come from all over Europe to give birth there. He really is the leading expert in alternative birthing practices.'

'Alternative birth?' Claire shook her head. 'Is it just me, Campbell, or has the whole world gone completely crazy? Surely things like inductions and Caesareans should be alternative birthing practices? What they call alternative these days is really just natural childbirth. When did it all get so screwed around?'

'I guess when doctors decided to interfere.'

'I'll drink to that.' She smiled and swallowed some of the rich, full-bodied wine.

'You'd get along so well with all my sisters.' His voice was laced with humour.

'All? How many do you have?'

'Four.'

'Wow.' Claire whistled. 'Let me guess. You're the youngest.'

'How did you know that?'

'You've obviously been spoilt and indulged. You certainly don't know how to take no for an answer.'

'Huh,' he snorted. 'You couldn't be further from the truth. More like harangued and henpecked.'

'Yeah, right.' Claire didn't believe a word of it.

'Well, maybe a little indulged. But mostly the h-words,' he answered sheepishly.

'Tell me about your family,' Claire said as the waiter placed their meals in front of them.

'Well…' He picked up his fork. 'My sisters, except for one, are nurses, two of them midwives. The other one's a GP. My mother is also a retired midwife. She's English and was a community midwife over there for many years. I think that's where I get my more modern approach from.'

'And your dad?'

'He died a few years ago. Heart attack.'

'Oh, Campbell.' Claire reached across and touched his hand. 'I'm so sorry.'

Campbell reeled from the look of compassion in her cinnamon eyes. She might be guarded most of the time but, hell, she could certainly be expressive. Something told him she knew a lot about grief. Would she open up to him? Was it worth the risk of seeing the shutters come down when her compassion gave her a whole new appeal?

'What about your family?'

Campbell felt the cool air against his hand as she abruptly removed hers, like a slap in the face. She returned her concentration to her meal and Campbell regretted having opened his mouth.

'Nothing to tell really. Nowhere near as colourful as your lot. Just Mum and Dad and me. Dad took early retirement a couple of years ago…for medical reasons.'

Campbell didn't dare ask about that. From the rigidness of her back he doubted she'd tell him anyway. They ate in silence for a little while, Campbell groping for a way to continue the conversation without her completely freezing him out.

'Have you always lived with them?'

'No. I moved back in a few years ago.' She placed her knife and fork down on her empty plate. 'Mmm, that was delicious.'

Campbell knew when to take a hint. 'Pleased you liked it. We'll have to come here again. Do you like sorbet? It's divine here. Better than anything you'll get in Italy.'

'Sorbet sounds perfect,' she agreed, and watched as he leaned back to beckon the waiter. His shirt pulled slightly out of his waistband. Claire tried really hard not to ogle but the tantalising glimpse of tanned skin gliding over muscle proved too much temptation. It certainly distracted her from the awkwardness she'd felt when he'd been quizzing her about her family and from his comment about them coming back here together.

Campbell placed their dessert order, aware the entire time of Claire's gaze. He felt his heart beat faster in anticipation. He looked at her and she didn't even bother to hide her hungry stare. He wanted her more now than he had since he'd first met her.

'Let's skip dessert,' he suggested softly, their gazes still entwined.

'Too late.' She gestured to the fast-approaching waiter.

'It's never too late.' His gaze didn't waver.

'I'm hungry.'

'So am I.'

Claire had no doubt as the waiter placed their plates before them that Campbell wasn't talking about the sorbet. Their desserts started to melt as their eye contact continued. The air between them grew thick with unspoken desire.

'You no like?' The waiter, completely oblivious to the raging atmosphere, interrupted their silent exchange.

'Oh, I like,' said Campbell, his eyes never leaving Claire's face. 'I like very much.'

Claire smiled at the waiter and rolled her eyes dramatically, assuring him that everything was fine. She picked up her spoon and took a mouthful of the tangy sorbet.

'Mmm, I think you're right. This definitely beats the sorbet I had in the Platz de San Marco in Venice. I didn't think that was possible.'

'Maybe it's the company.'

'Maybe.'

The evening air was balmy as they stepped outside twenty minutes later.

'Why don't you come back to my place for a coffee?' Campbell kept his voice light.

'Oh, Campbell, I don't think that's a very good idea. I've had a lovely evening but I think I should go home.' Claire was surprised at how badly she wanted to go with him. Still, that didn't make it wise.

'No strings, I promise. I've got this great home video of a footling breech I delivered while I was in France. I thought you might be interested.'

'A footling?'

'Ever seen one?'

'No. We just don't deliver them any more.'

'It's fantastic footage,' he coaxed.

'OK,' she agreed slowly, and smiled. Sure, why not? It sounded interesting. Claire knew it was a probably just an excuse to spend more time with her, but she was an adult. Whatever his motive, she was there to watch the video, make some polite conversation and then leave. Nothing was going to happen. She was sure she could keep her hormones in check for an hour or so.

'I'll drive you,' he suggested, holding out his hand.

'No. I'll follow you in my car.'

'I really thought you were going to do a runner,' Campbell told her as he inserted his key into the front door.

'Oh, ye of little faith,' she mocked him playfully as she stepped into his apartment. He switched the lights on then dimmed them to a soft glow. Claire wandered over to the bank of huge floor-to-ceiling glass windows offering a spectacular view of the river and the city skyline.

'Wow! Nice digs,' she complimented him as he clattered around in the kitchen, fixing coffee.

'Yes, I was really lucky to find it,' he said, carrying a tray to the lounge area where the television rested in a beautiful heavy wooden cabinet. He placed the coffee-mugs on a matching low table and indicated for Claire to sit beside him on a double-seater leather lounge chair.

She sat sipping her coffee, watching his jeans pull and strain across his taut bottom as he found the tape and placed it in the machine. She tried not to look but, hell, he was sexy!

He smiled at her as he sat beside her and pushed the play button on the remote. She dragged her gaze from him with difficulty as the screen flickered to life and the low moans of a woman in labour commanded her attention.

For the next fifteen minutes Claire watched, intrigued, as Campbell deftly guided the couple through the birth of their baby. He supplied a low commentary from time to time and when Claire saw the first foot hang free from the birth canal she was totally involved and in awe of Campbell's cool and professionalism.

Despite the risks, the baby was delivered without a hitch and Claire felt tears prick her eyes as the emotional couple embraced Campbell and wept openly. She was touched by his handling of the sentimental moment and somehow wasn't surprised to see his eyes shimmer with tears as he held the newborn he had helped into the world.

'That was beautiful, Campbell,' Claire said, blinking rapidly as the screen went blank.

'It was one of the most incredible experiences of my life,' he admitted quietly.

She stood before she was tempted to turn and look at him. They were a little too close on the lounge for comfort. After witnessing such an emotional scene, Claire didn't trust her reactions.

'Why don't you open the doors and go out onto the deck?' Campbell suggested softly. 'I'll bring us out a drink.'

The fresh air hit Claire's heated skin like an arctic blast. She sucked in deep, cleansing breaths, waiting for her heart rate to settle. She had to get out of here. Seeing Campbell all dewy-eyed with the naked, wet newborn had started Claire's thoughts on a path she didn't want to go down. She had to leave. Now.

He crossed to where she stood on the far corner of the deck, her hands gripping the railing, her back to him. He drew closer until he could feel the nervous heat radiating from her body. He was careful not to touch her, ignoring the urge to pull her against him.

'Port,' he murmured quietly, and watched her shoulders tense as she turned to face him.

'Th-thanks.' OK. One drink and then she'd leave.

Claire sipped at the warm liquid and felt its fiery residue trail a path all the way to her stomach. She looked into the glass, swishing the liquid around and watching it coat the sides of the glass.

He stood beside her, sipping his own drink. Nearly touching. Nearly.

'Claire…' he murmured, his voice deep and throaty. He turned to face her and the breeze enveloped him in her scent. 'God, you smell incredible,' he groaned as he closed the small space separating them and nuzzled her hair. He inhaled the exotic aroma of her shampoo and felt himself tighten.

Claire swallowed as his nuzzling sent the most delicious sensations crawling along her scalp.

'I really must go,' she croaked, desperately trying to fight the fog of desire and sound like she meant it.

'OK,' he whispered, as his lips travelled to the sensitive skin of her neck where he continued to nuzzle up and down the slope of her neck and along the slant of her shoulder as far as the fabric of her dress would allow.

Claire shut her eyes tight and felt herself swaying into Campbell. She wasn't sure if she made it all the way by herself or if he met her halfway. Her thought processes were beginning to blur as her skin broke out in goose-bumps and her abdominal muscles contracted with desire.

She felt the hardness of his erection immediately. Her toes curled as she heard his swift intake of breath. He pressed his lips into her neck just below her ear and gave a groan that conveyed pleasure and pain.

'Don't do that,' she begged passionately. 'I can't do this,' she panted. 'We have to stop.'

Campbell drew back, his chest heaving. 'Are you sure?' he asked, and his eyes conveyed the pure sexual agony he was feeling.

'I shouldn't...'

'But you want to?'

Claire watched, mesmerised, as his lips descended slowly towards hers. He was taking his time, giving her time to back out, but she was rooted to the spot, hypnotised by the magic she knew his lips would unleash.

She sighed softly as his mouth gently touched hers. She needed this kiss like she needed her next breath. She opened her mouth and it was all the encouragement he needed.

Claire matched his ardour, one intoxicating kiss following another. The solid wall of his body pinned Claire back against the railing. He used the position to his advantage, rubbing his pelvis long and hard and slow against hers, placing the most exquisite pressure on the sensitive flesh beneath her dress. She cried out for mercy, sure that she was about to break into a thousand pieces from the pleasure.

'Let's go inside,' he suggested raggedly, sweeping her up into his arms.

Claire wrapped her arms around his neck and kissed him again. Deep, wet, delicious kisses. If she'd been at all aware of her surroundings she would have admired the way Campbell strode through the apartment, blindly navigating his way past furniture and through rooms, not once breaking contact with her lips.

They tumbled onto his bed and Claire felt his hands glide the zip of her dress down. She was suddenly consumed with the urge to be rid of it. She pushed him aside and stood beside the bed. One shrug of her shoulders and the red linen slipped to the floor.

Claire stood before Campbell in her black lacy hipster knickers and black lacy camisole. The two wispy pieces of satin didn't quite meet, her flat midriff bare to his hungry gaze.

Claire thought, rather belatedly, that she should feel shy, standing in front of him practically naked. But when he sat up, perched on the edge of the bed and whistled appreciatively, all she could feel was pride.

'Are you sure about this?'

Claire nodded. Right or wrong, she couldn't deny her body this. His kisses had woken the part of her that had slumbered for too many years.

She crossed her arms in front of her and grasped the fabric of her camisole, about to pull it over her head, when Campbell placed a restraining hand on her arm.

'No,' he stated. 'I want to take them off.'

He pulled her to him, his head level with her stomach, his mouth finding the bare skin of her middle, his tongue dipping into her belly button. His hands pushed under the silky fabric and slowly ascended her ribs, taking the camisole with him.

When they reached her breasts, Claire gasped and clutched his shoulders as he rubbed the already fully aroused nipples. Whoever had said there was a fine line between pleasure and pain had sure known what they were talking about. It was exquisite torture.

His hands left her breasts and in one swift movement he pulled the scrap of material over her head and flung it across the room. Her breasts swung free into his eager palms, quickly replaced by his even more eager mouth.

Claire felt a jolt of desire stab low in her pelvis and radiate further until it tingled between her legs. The friction of her lacy knickers against her engorged flesh was almost too erotic to bear.

Campbell's mouth laved every inch of her breasts, tugging and sucking at the nipples until they were hard and elongated with need. He had turned her body into one giant, exposed nerve, hypersensitive to his every touch. She couldn't think. She couldn't talk. All she was capable of was holding on and groaning monosyllabic primal noises as her body dissolved in a vortex of pleasure.

She didn't even register him pulling her underwear down to her knees until she felt his fingers gently probing the tingling flesh at the apex of her thighs. She cried out loud and clutched at his shoulders when she felt one, then two fingers enter her. He repeated the motion rhythmically as his thumb found the swollen nub it was seeking and moved in sync to the tempo set by his fingers. In, out, round and round.

Claire's head fell back as a maelstrom of sensations stormed through her. Her fingers sliced through his hair, hanging on for dear life as she felt her legs give way. He adjusted his position slightly to support her weight, never breaking his rhythm.

He picked up the pace, her desperate cries urging him on. Her hands imprisoned his head against her breasts as a pressure of intense proportions built rapidly in her core. It spread outwards, its tentacles stretching to all her muscles, tensing them to an almost unbearable rigidity. It paralysed her diaphragm, her breath stuttering out in short hiccupy blasts.

Claire heard herself cry out his name, begging him for

release. And just when she thought she'd explode, it happened. Her spine arched, her head flung back and an animalistic groan escaped from her open, gasping mouth. She clung to Campbell like flotsam in a swirling, cyclone-tossed sea, grateful to him for holding her up and for the pleasure that battered her like torrential rain.

Campbell held on tight as she rode the crest of her climax, his breathing as ragged as hers. He felt her muscles clench against his fingers still buried inside her. He felt each contraction and revelled in the knowledge that he was responsible.

As he held her body, still quivering in the aftermath, he was amazed at how she'd given herself so completely, especially after her earlier reticence.

'Claire?' He eased her away slightly, wanting to look into her eyes. 'Are you OK?' Her flushed face and glazed eyes spoke volumes. She certainly looked OK. More than OK.

Claire moved out of his embrace, stepping out of her not quite removed knickers, and collapsed on the bed, her glazed vision coming to rest on the ceiling. Had what had just happened really happened to her? Even now, minutes later, she could still feel the odd ripple undulate through her muscles deep inside.

'Claire?' Campbell's voice intruded on her musings. She turned her head as he lowered himself back so their faces were level. Their gazes met, her brown eyes still a little glazed. His were greener than green. Irish eyes. So expressive. So green. They screamed meadows and shamrocks.

'Wow,' she whispered, raising her hand to push his fringe back off his forehead.

Campbell laughed, a deep hearty noise. Claire joined

him. It was easier to laugh than to try and wrap her head around what had just transpired.

Gradually their mirth subsided, leaving them staring into each other's eyes again.

'Campbell, I…' Claire groped for the right words to express her wonder.

'Shh,' he ordered quietly, placing his fingers against her ravaged mouth. 'Don't say anything.'

Claire felt a tingle in her lips beneath his fingers and was suddenly aware of her nakedness. The air cooling her skin was the merest of caresses.

Campbell noticed the change in her eyes immediately. The glaze cleared, to be replaced by the flame of rekindled desire. His pulse, which had only just settled, picked up again. His breathing became shallower.

Her lips pressed together, laying a gentle kiss against his fingers. Such a sweet, almost innocent thing for her to do, especially given what had just happened. But his reaction to it was swift and definitely not innocent. His erection, still the same one from the deck, raged against the confines of his zipper, almost bursting free.

'I think you're a bit overdressed, Dr Deane,' she whispered, and Campbell groaned as she vaulted up and straddled him all in one smooth movement.

If he'd thought she'd looked magnificent before, nothing prepared him for this view. Gloriously naked, sitting astride him, her breasts jutting, nipples dark, still engorged from his earlier attentions.

She pressed her hips down onto his denim-clad erection, smiling knowingly. She rubbed herself against him as she threw her head back, revelling in her power.

She leaned closer to him so her mouth was mere millimetres from his, her breasts touching the rough fabric of his shirt. She rubbed them slowly against the material, kissing his mouth simultaneously.

He felt her low moan against his lips as it escaped hers. She lifted her mouth and grinned wickedly at him. He smiled back, wondering what was going on inside her head to give her that smug look. She shifted slightly, presenting a breast to his mouth, just out of reach. Campbell licked his lips, his throat suddenly as dry as the Sahara.

Campbell groaned as Claire slowly, bit by bit, lowered herself into his mouth. He sucked greedily the second he felt her puckered flesh nudge his lips. He missed her sharp intake of breath as his moan of satisfaction rumbled through his head.

She tasted so good it was suddenly too much for Campbell. He grasped her hips and ground them against his erection. He heard her cry out as she continued his action, writhing against him. It felt incredible. Her breast in his mouth and her pelvis rocking into his. He dug his fingers into her buttocks, encouraging her to continue.

'We really must do something about these clothes,' she murmured, as she tugged at the hem of his shirt, yanked it up over his head and flung it across the room, where it joined her camisole.

Campbell found her proximity too hard to ignore as his hands caressed her back and his lips sought the elegant length of her neck. He wanted to taste every inch of her.

'Nuh-uh,' she admonished, wagging her finger at him as she pushed him backwards gently. He reached for her again and she slapped his hand away playfully. Campbell thought he was going to lose his mind. He had to touch her.

'Claire,' he groaned. Campbell wasn't at all sure he could last the distance. He felt ready to erupt at any second.

She opened her eyes and grinned that wicked grin.

'Temptress,' he accused. His voice trembled with desire.

She laughed and pushed herself off him, hushing his complaint. 'Still too many clothes,' she said, and reached for his zipper.

Campbell hastily lifted his hips off the bed, and as she divested him first of the denim and then his cotton underwear. He suppressed the urge to groan out loud as his erection finally sprang free of its cloth prison.

Campbell sat up and tried to drag Claire closer.

'Nuh-uh.' She shook her head and then knelt in front of him, kissing him full and deep and long on the lips. Campbell felt the blood rush through his veins as the heat from the kiss burned a hole in his stomach lining.

'Claire,' he said urgently, pulling her off him to look into her eyes. It was almost his undoing, seeing them drunk with passion, her mouth swollen and moist from kissing him. They stared at each other, their harsh breathing the only noise in the room.

He kissed her again roughly, plundering her mouth. 'I want it to be perfect the first time. I want to be inside you. I want to feel you around me.'

He watched her as she considered his words for a moment.

'OK.'

Campbell fell back on the bed, bringing her with him until she once again straddled him. He clutched her hips and surrendered to the sensation of her lithe naked body lowering itself onto him. Campbell groaned as bit by bit she swallowed his erection into her tight, moist depth.

He heard a corresponding moan and he pulled out and plunged in again just to hear it once more. She didn't disappoint him. Each moan from her enticed him to plunge again, deeper and harder.

Campbell knew he was coming almost from the first time he entered her. He pushed it aside and held it off for as long as possible, but when he heard Claire's escalating cries and felt her begin to contract around him, he knew he was spiralling out of control.

He gripped her thighs, his fingers digging into the tanned skin. His body tensed and then bucked and reared as his climax erupted.

Their cries rose and mingled as their separate orgasms became one.

CHAPTER FIVE

CLAIRE woke at 4.30 to the first signs of the encroaching dawn. Campbell's hand rested, heavy and warm, on her flat stomach. She looked into his face, relaxed in slumber, his hair flopping in his eyes, and remembered how it had looked last night, animated with passion. She suppressed the urge to kiss his, oh so tempting mouth. That would probably wake him, and Claire had to get going.

Her mother would be awake in an hour and it was imperative that she be home. Claire always tried to be there first thing, to attend to her mother's personal needs. It allowed her father, who got up twice a night to change Mary's position, to get as much sleep as possible before he began his long day caring for his wife. It also preserved her dignity—what was left of it.

As she gazed on Campbell's sleeping face, her heart contracted with an emotion too frightening to analyse. Thinking about her mother was just the bucket of cold water she needed to bring her back to reality. Last night had been a mistake. She should have been stronger.

It wasn't fair to become involved with him when she knew that one day she might end up like her mother. She didn't want Campbell to have to go through what her father was now going through—no one should have to.

And what if he didn't want to? Shane had wasted no time in leaving after the bombshell had hit. And he had been in love with her—supposedly. She couldn't bear being rejected like that again.

And what about Campbell's desire to have children and

his feelings about bringing children into the world when a genetic illness existed? Her decision to remain childless would deny him the baby he yearned for, and he'd made it quite plain that he wouldn't want one with mutant genes anyway.

No. It was better this way. There were too many reasons they couldn't be together. Claire gently removed his arm and slid out from under the sheet. She gathered her clothes in the semi-gloom and quickly put them on. Campbell didn't stir. It took every ounce of her self-control to walk away.

Campbell knew the instant he woke up that he was alone. Somehow he wasn't surprised. Disappointed was a better word. Being with Claire had been fantastic. Not just the sex. It was about more than that. Snuggling close as they'd drifted off to sleep had somehow seemed natural. Right. It would have been perfect to have woken up and been able to reach out and touch her. Talk to her. Tell her he loved her.

Yes, Campbell thought, rolling onto his back, he loved her. There was no sense denying it or trying to wrap it up any other way. Holding her, kissing her, making love to her last night had cemented his realisation. He had fallen for her hard. He basked in the truth.

But did she love him? Somehow he suspected that it was still too early in their relationship for Claire. So could she, or rather would she, allow herself to love him, too?

The afterglow that he'd woken with was starting to fade as the questions kept coming. How should he proceed? What he wanted to do was make a huge romantic declaration. He loved her and he wanted to share his feelings with her. Hell, he wanted to shout it to the world.

But the sensible part of him urged caution. It had been

a long, hard slog getting her to agree to a date, and that had only eventuated because he'd shamelessly taken advantage of her at a weak moment. Getting her to fall in love with him was a big call.

Campbell acknowledged he was going to have to be patient. Not one of his best traits. But if that's what it required, he was willing to give it a go. He'd woo her slowly, subtly, and before she knew it she'd be declaring her undying love. He needed a plan.

He puzzled over it for a few minutes, formulating a recipe for success. Yes, he mused, it was all about the three Ps. Patience. Persistence. Presence. The last one particularly. It would be important to see her as much as possible. Show her the time of her life, make her see what she'd been missing all these years.

Not just lots of sex, although that'd be nice. No. It was about more than that. It was about having fun together, laughing, talking, sharing. Lovers' stuff. And no pressure. Just always being there until she couldn't recall what life had been like without him. Until she said those three little words.

'Good morning, Shirley,' Claire greeted the new mother as she entered the room.

'Hello, Claire. Goodness, what have you been up to? You're glowing!'

Claire blushed. She felt like she'd been caught with her hand in the cookie jar.

'You should talk.' She grinned at her client. 'I could see your I've-just-had-a-baby glow from the car park.'

Shirley laughed and Claire breathed a sigh of relief that she'd successfully turned the conversation back to Shirley.

'Davy get you up much?'

'A few times,' Shirley confirmed.

'Is he feeding well?' Claire sat on the edge of the bed and stroked the sleeping baby's head.

'Seems to be. He's attached much better than the other three ever did. Maybe I've finally got the hang of it.' She laughed.

'Where's Graham? Didn't he stay?'

'No, he went home with the kids early last night. He'll be back to pick me up around lunchtime. That should be OK, shouldn't it?'

'Don't see why not.' Claire smiled. 'Why don't you put him down and I'll check how you're doing?'

Shirley placed the sleeping baby in his clear plastic crib and lay down on the bed. Claire took her temperature, pulse and blood pressure and then gently palpated Shirley's abdomen.

'Tummy's going down nicely,' Claire confirmed. 'How's your loss?'

'Still heavy,' said Shirley, used to such personal questions.

'Any afterpains?'

'Initially, yes! But Graham got me a hot pack, which helped. They're a bloody nuisance. After all you go through with labour, you'd think that'd be it but, oh, no!'

Claire smiled and agreed with Shirley. Some women, more commonly those who were on their second or subsequent babies, found these pains, caused by the contracting uterus, even worse than labour. Most found them uncomfortable, like heavy period pains, but a few even needed pain relief when they occurred.

'Well, I'll have whoever's on call for Paediatrics come and check little Davy over, and then you should be able to go.'

'What about his day-three heel prick? Will they do that at the clinic?'

'You can, but the hospital has a community midwife service that can do that for you. I'll call them on Monday and they'll come out to your home and do the heel prick there. You'll also be able to talk to them about any concerns.'

Claire left Shirley to shower and pack. She wandered into the kitchen and made herself a cup of tea, her mind completely preoccupied with the events of last night. She took the tea into her office and sat down at her desk, staring absently out the window.

She worried her bottom lip as snippets of their conversation and flashes of their love-making came to her unbidden. It had been a wonderful evening. Perfect in every way. Except for the fact that it should never have happened.

Goodness only knew what Campbell was thinking about it all. Would he assume there was more to come? Would he expect that? She could hardly blame him if he did. What if he thought they were now a couple?

Claire took a sip of her lukewarm tea. Had she really been staring into space that long? She put her cup down and firmly pushed her thoughts aside. She had a lot to do to organise Shirley's and Davy's discharge.

She made a note in her diary for Monday to organise with the community midwifery service a home visit to Shirley. Next, she paged the paediatric registrar covering for the weekend. He answered promptly and agreed to come straight away. Claire collected the paperwork together, writing her own notes and filling in the discharge form.

'Hi, Claire.'

She'd been so preoccupied with her work she hadn't heard the swing doors open. 'Hi, William. I was so pleased when it was you who answered the page.'

Dr William Casey and Claire had known each other for many years. They had a good relationship, which had flourished, despite her rejection of his advances when they'd first met. He was very easygoing and had taken it in his stride.

'Only one more year of this awful shift work and then private practice here I come.'

Claire laughed. William had wanted to be a paediatrician for ever and had been steadily working towards that goal.

'You're not selling out, are you?' she mocked.

'Claire, Claire, Claire,' he tsked. 'You really have problems with the establishment, don't you?'

'Nah. Getting too old for that now.' She laughed.

William stood up straighter in the doorway, his eyes narrowing, speculation causing them to gleam.

'Something's not right,' he mused. 'You look…different.'

'Different?' she enquired, trying not to blush. 'I don't know what you're talking about.'

'Yes, you look like you've just been… Oh, my God! He did it, didn't he? He won. He wore you down. Campbell, the old dog! Well, well, well.'

'Don't be ridiculous, William,' Claire blustered, trying to look affronted.

'Oh, I see. Not going to kiss and tell, huh? Don't worry, Claire, your secret is safe with me.'

'William,' Claire sighed. 'You're the biggest gossip this hospital has ever known.'

'Yeah, you're right. Guess that's bad luck for you.' He laughed at her unimpressed face. 'Got a baby for me?'

Claire was grateful for the change of subject and led him in to Shirley before she succumbed to the urge to throttle him.

A gossip he might be, but a more thorough doctor was hard to find. 'Sorry to disturb you, little mate,' he whispered to the baby as he picked him up out of his cot and unwrapped him.

Davy opened sleep-bleary eyes but didn't look too cranky at the intrusion. Even when William flashed a torch in his eyes, checking for the red reflex of the cornea, he didn't object. William assessed all five reflexes that newborns should have, and then flipped him on his tummy. He visually inspected, as well as physically checked, by running his finger down, Davy's spine to make sure it was complete.

Davy did object when William performed the test for clicky hips. He howled and went a very impressive shade of red as William applied pressure through his little bent knees down into the hip joint.

'Sorry, little mate,' he soothed, rubbing the newborn's tummy as he checked that both testicles were descended.

'Good time for a feed,' said Shirley. 'If you've finished?' she asked.

'Sure,' William agreed. 'Nothing like a full stomach after such a harrowing experience, hey, little man?' William crooned as he handed Davy to his mother.

'Has he passed urine yet?'

'Several times,' Shirley confirmed.

'Any meconium yet?'

'Oh, yes!' Shirley laughed. 'I've saved it for you if you want to check.' She laughed again. Having done this for the fourth time, Shirley knew that black, tarry bowel motions were best left alone.

Mercifully William didn't stay on after he passed little Davy for discharge. He left straight away but did manage a lewd wink at Claire before he shut the door.

She escaped to her office, once again cursing under her breath. Great, it was going to be around the hospital in five minutes flat. Of that Claire had no doubt. By the time

Campbell got to work on Monday it'd be so blown out of proportion they'd be practically married. So much for one night of passion. No one was going to believe that was the extent of it.

Oh, well, Claire decided, rearranging the stuff on her desk, she'd weathered years of St Jude's gossip before. She could do it again. Once people realised that she and Campbell weren't an item, the talk would die down and be completely snuffed out once a juicier titbit came along.

Claire heard Shirley's family arrive and went out to greet them. Graham had brought the other three kids and they were all very excited, jostling to be the first to hold their new baby brother.

While Graham supervised the children, Claire finalised things with Shirley.

'Now, page me if there are any problems. That's what I'm here for—all right?'

'Sure thing,' Shirley agreed, as she signed the discharge papers.

'Here's your appointment for your six-week check,' said Claire, handing the card to her. 'Expect a phone call on Monday about the heel prick. I'll see you in six weeks, but remember—'

'I know, any problems and you'll be the first to know. I promise.'

'Good.' Claire grinned as she accepted Shirley's hug of gratitude.

She saw them out the door. It was quite a noisy goodbye and Claire was still smiling when she shut the door and started on the clean-up in Shirley's room.

Claire was making the bed, her last chore, when she heard the swing doors open.

'Hello. Anyone here?'

Campbell's voice reached out and touched her, even

from the other side of the wall. She groaned inwardly. She wasn't ready to face him just yet. She hadn't had enough time to work out what to say to him.

She knew what had to be said but hadn't anticipated how difficult it would be to face him so soon after having seen him naked. After he'd seen her naked. How could you tell someone that one night of mind-blowing sex was it and expect them to believe you? Because that was what she had to say. There could be no more.

Claire contemplated hiding somewhere, quickly scanning the room for a good position, but discarded the idea just as quickly. How juvenile! Never put off till tomorrow what you could do today. Right? She took a deep breath and went out to him.

'Hi,' she said quietly, coming to a halt in the doorway. She leaned against the doorframe, feeling weak from her reaction to his presence. He was in casual mode again, looking even more delicious than last night, kind of rumpled and content. Damn her weak body! Claire had to grind her shoes into the floor to stop herself running into his arms.

'Hi, yourself.' He smiled.

They stared greedily for the longest time. Campbell moved towards her, reaching out. She very nearly gave in to the temptation. Heaven knew, she wanted to feel his body against hers so badly she ached.

But at the last moment sanity prevailed and she backed away from him into the room. It didn't matter how much her body ached, she had to think with her head. There were things to say.

She crossed back to the bed and picked up the sheet, busying herself. Claire could feel the intensity of his gaze fill the distance between them.

'I missed you this morning.' His quiet voice broke into her activity.

'Help me with this?' She nodded for him to get the other side.

He crossed until he was opposite her. One bed and ten years of baggage between them.

'We need to talk.' Claire fussed, getting the corners just right as she spoke. 'I'm really sorry—'

'Please, don't say you're sorry last night happened.'

'No. Campbell, I don't mean… I'm not sorry about last night. I should be. I shouldn't have let it happen, but…it did and, no, I'm not sorry.'

'Oh, Claire.' Campbell sat down heavily on the half-made bed, a sigh of relief escaping his lips. 'Don't do that to me.'

'What I was going to say,' she said, sitting down on her side, 'was that I'm sorry but the cat is out of the bag. As far as the hospital grapevine goes anyway.'

'Already?' Campbell whistled. 'How did that happen? Were they looking through the keyhole?'

'No.' Claire laughed. 'William Casey came and did the discharge check on little Davy. He guessed.'

'Guessed?'

'Yeah, I know. Crazy, isn't it? He reckoned I looked different and put two and two together.'

'Well, you do have that thoroughly kissed look.'

'I…I do?' Claire pressed a hand to her mouth.

'Very much.'

Claire's eyes dilated as his hungry gaze followed the movement of her hand to her lips. She felt as if a hand had grabbed her insides and was squeezing. She heard the texture of his breathing roughen and felt hers fall into sync.

'It doesn't matter anyway, Claire. Let them talk. Our relationship is our business.'

Claire stood up and moved over to the window. He'd just mentioned the R-word. This was what she had feared would happen. She sensed things would get out of hand if she didn't put a stop to his fanciful thoughts right now. One roll in the hay did not a relationship make. Right?

'It matters to me, Campbell.'

'Why?'

'Because…it was just one night.' She turned to face him. 'We don't have a relationship. Last night was great. But wrong. I'm sorry if us sleeping together led you to believe differently. It shouldn't have happened and it's not going to happen again.'

'How do you know that?'

'Because I'm not going to let it. I seriously don't know what came over me last night, Campbell. But it doesn't negate the reasons I have for not dating or getting involved. They still exist.'

'So, what was last night, then?'

'Last night was a serious error in judgement. A very pleasant one but…I guess I just didn't expect to be so swept away. It's been such a long time for me…'

'So you used me last night?' He stood and paced and Claire didn't need to look at him to know he was angry.

'No. It wasn't like that!'

'No? Seems to me I was a convenient body to ease years of sexual frustration.'

Claire felt wounded by Campbell's unfair judgement of her. She had obviously hurt him, but he knew how to wound her just as effectively.

'Look, we went on a date. I was very attracted to you—'

'I know the feeling.'

'I wasn't thinking about the future. I wasn't thinking at all. We were kissing and one thing led to another and… I was just feeling, Campbell. I wasn't thinking. I never promised you a relationship. I never promised you a happily ever after.'

'Well, pardon me if I assumed certain things while you were half-crazy with lust last night.' His voice was icy.

'Lust, Campbell. Lust. You said it.'

'I didn't think you were that kind of woman.'

Claire's head snapped up as his accusation hit home.

'What? You mean the kind who indiscriminately sleeps with someone and then dumps them the next day? I'm sorry, I forgot that was a man's prerogative.'

Campbell stopped pacing and pushed his hands through his hair. 'I'm sorry,' he said placatingly, rubbing his eyes. 'That was unforgivable. Claire…I just want to be with you. Let me be with you,'

'I don't want to be with you,' she said, turning away from him so he couldn't see the lie reflected in her expression.

'You're a liar.' His voice was calm. Emotionless.

'Just go, Campbell,' she said quietly.

'This isn't over, Claire,' he warned. 'Every time your head hits your pillow, you're going to be thinking about me. About me inside you. I hope it drives you mad. As mad as it's going drive me.'

Claire heard his footsteps retreat and it took all her willpower to stand her ground. Her arms shook with the effort of keeping them firmly planted on the window-sill. She would not call him back. It was better this way.

Later that day, Claire found herself back at the birth centre with another of her clients in labour.

The birth stretched into the night and she paged Barbara Willis, the night-shift midwife, to tell her not to bother coming in as she would stay until her patient had delivered.

Finally around three a.m. the tiny baby boy made its

entry into the world, much to Claire's delight and the mother's relief. Baby Jonathon slept on obliviously as Claire fussed around, settling him into the mobile crib.

The first embers of dawn were glowing in the heavens when Claire finally left St Jude's. She yawned as she pushed open the front door. Two nights with little sleep had really taken their toll. But her work wasn't over yet.

Claire poked her head into her mother's room. She was awake, as Claire knew she would be. 'Hello, Mum,' Claire said softly. She opened the curtains to admit the early morning sunshine. 'How about I read you the paper and then I wash your hair?'

The pump that delivered hourly metered doses of a special nutritional formula into her mother's feeding tube beeped that it was empty, and Claire switched it off. She opened the newspaper that had been on the front lawn and thumbed through it with one hand and stroked her mother's hand with the other. Claire picked out stories she felt would interest her mother…had once interested her anyway.

She looked into her mother's vacant, staring eyes. Who knew what went on inside her head any more? Speech had been difficult for a few years and non-existent for a year now. Did she understand? Claire wanted to believe that she did.

One thing was for sure, seeing her mother like this re-inforced her reasons for rejecting Campbell. She'd definitely done the right thing.

Campbell… Would he be awake yet? Would he still be mad with her? Spending time with her mother like this always left her feeling flat. It was like looking into a mirror. She was scared for her mother and anxious of what would become of her father after…

It would have been so nice to go to Campbell, crawl into

bed beside him and have him hold her until all her fears went away. To confide in him.

She shook herself. What was wrong with her? Surely years of denial had annihilated such temptations? Had sleeping with Campbell triggered these feelings? She should have known it'd be more complicated than just two people having sex. Intimacy was never that straightforward—that's why she had avoided it!

She pushed these confusing thoughts aside as she lifted Mary onto the mobile shower chair with ease. Years of nursing had taught her to lift properly and, despite the nightly supplements, her mother had wasted away to practically nothing in the last year.

The *en suite* bathroom had been modified as her mother had become more dependent, so there was ample room for Claire to shower her mother and wash her hair. She chatted as she saw to her hygiene needs, prattling on about baby Jonathon and baby David.

Claire yearned to tell her about Campbell. Confide in her mother as daughters the world over usually did. But something held her back. Telling her mother made it seem like they were involved. And they weren't.

All these thoughts whirred around in Claire's head as she finally collapsed into bed a couple of hours later. Fortunately they weren't enough to halt the pressing need for sleep. She closed her eyes and for the first time in a long time it was not her mother she dreamed about as sleep claimed her. It was Campbell.

CHAPTER SIX

CAMPBELL had no sooner sat down at his desk on Monday morning than the phone rang. It was Martin with a command, poorly disguised as a request, to see him immediately in his office.

Replacing the phone, Campbell decided that Martin could wait until he was good and ready. He'd head up there in a few minutes. He was in no mood to be ordered around, particularly by a pompous fool like Martin.

He drummed his fingers on the desk and then stood abruptly, stalking to the window. He stared with unseeing eyes at the phenomenal view.

Snatches of the incredible experience with Claire on Friday night chased snippets of their argument on Saturday morning around and around his head. So much for the three Ps. If she refused to see him again, his plan would be down the gurgler.

He'd wanted to shake her on Saturday. Grab hold of her arms and shake her until she understood that he loved her and they were wasting precious time, arguing. Time that they could spend loving each other.

Not for the first time, Campbell wished he knew what was eating her. Why did she persist with her no-relationship mantra? Why couldn't she open up to him? Had Shane hurt her that badly? No. She seemed to be way over that—there had to be something more.

He reluctantly made his way up to the executive offices, still deep in thought. The lift opened just as Campbell was coming to an important decision. Whatever her reasons, they were irrelevant. His objective was still the same—to make Claire West his. If one night of passion wasn't enough to sway her, then he'd have to go back to basics again.

He heard the raised voices coming from Martin's office from out in the hallway. He quickened his pace as he realised that one of them belonged to Claire.

Campbell burst through the door just as Martin was saying, 'If it's the last thing I do, I'm going to see that centre shut down.'

'Morning, all,' he said cheerfully, entering the fray.

Martin shot him an irritated look. Claire had murder in her eyes. Her look of relief as she realised it was him was heart-warming. Campbell cautioned himself not to get too caught up by it. She was probably only grateful that his arrival had stopped her from strangling Martin with his own necktie and spending the rest of her life in prison. The cleaner would probably have been given the same treatment.

Hell, she looks tired, he thought. He knew he shouldn't be, but he was secretly pleased that sleep hadn't come easily to her either. Good. He'd hate to think he was the only one suddenly afflicted with insomnia.

'So pleased you could join us.' Martin's sarcastic comment intruded on Campbell's thoughts.

Deciding to let that one slip by, Campbell guessed that calm and reason was definitely lacking in their conversation. Luckily, he was very good at calm and reason.

'Is there a problem here?'

'You could say that,' snorted Martin. 'Were you aware that Sister West delivered a breech baby at the centre on Friday afternoon?'

'Yes.'

'Were you aware that this contravenes the birth centre

protocol? A protocol that Sister West herself implemented?'

'Yes.'

'This is exactly what I feared would happen. Give them some autonomy and she takes it upon herself to risk the life of a mother and her baby, all in the name of natural birth.'

'I don't think that's entirely fair, Martin.' Calm and reason.

'Fair! Fair? How fair would it have been if complications had developed and the baby had died? They would have sued us from here to breakfast-time, and quite rightly, too.'

'The baby didn't die.' Claire tried to keep the exasperation from her voice.

'Lucky.'

'No, not lucky. Educated.'

'Oh…you think you know more than me, Sister West? I've been delivering babies for nearly forty years. Your experience is nothing next to mine.'

'Now, wait a minute—' Campbell interjected.

'Campbell, I don't need you to defend me,' she snapped. 'If Martin could just listen for a minute instead of ranting and raving—'

'I have not ranted or raved,' he blustered.

'Martin, I haven't been able to get a word in edgewise since I got here.'

Martin glared at her and sat down huffily.

'Firstly, I made every attempt to get Shirley to Labour Ward but that baby wanted out. Would you rather she gave birth in the lift or a corridor?'

'I think anything is preferable to delivering it yourself.'

'I am perfectly capable of delivering a breech baby. I've delivered more than my fair share. I assessed the patient and I assessed the risks. I'm a good midwife, Martin. You may have more years than me but it doesn't negate my experience. Quite frankly, I'm insulted that you would think so.'

Campbell sat back and watched Martin squirm. She was doing it again. Making a speech. Just like the first day he had met her. And his body was as predictable as ever. Man, how did she do this to him?

She was standing her ground, stabbing the air with her finger to emphasise her points. Her brown eyes boiled like hot mud pools and her chest rose and fell quickly, sucking in much-needed oxygen for her brain to formulate her next words.

His brain, on the other hand, was suffering from the usual reduction of oxygen as all the blood rushed to another part of his anatomy. Stop this! Rhetoric shouldn't be sexy. Heaven help him.

'Secondly, a complete novice could have delivered that baby. We really did nothing. He all but delivered himself.'

'We?' Martin queried, sitting forward.

'Yes, we. Campbell was at the centre when Shirley arrived.'

'You were there?' Martin demanded.

'I've been trying to tell you that from the minute you hauled me in here,' Claire snapped.

'And is that your assessment?' Martin asked Campbell. 'There was no time to get the patient to Labour Ward?'

Campbell noticed Claire bristling, drawing herself up to launch another verbal attack. 'I absolutely agree with Claire. Little Davy's bottom was well and truly out.'

'Well, if you feel it was an unavoidable situation, I shall just have to trust your judgement.'

'It'd be nice just once to enjoy the same trust.' Claire's icy voice conveyed her displeasure. Campbell caught the irritated look she shot him. Even that wasn't enough to dampen his raging response.

Martin chose to ignore her. 'I want written incident reports on my desk about this by the end of the week from both of you. And I still intend to make a full report to the board.'

'Well, you do what you have to do, Dr Shaw,' Claire said wearily. 'I've got a centre to run.'

Claire was too exhausted to even slam the door after her. Too tired to acknowledge how wonderful it had been to have Campbell on her side. She'd expected to feel awkwardness after their argument on Saturday, but she was honestly too tired to care.

She couldn't remember ever having felt so tired. The adrenaline that had been pumping around her system during their heated discussion had left her feeling even more depleted. All she wanted was to get out of there. She could almost feel her mattress beneath her.

If only it wasn't this morning she so desperately needed sleep. Mary went to respite care until mid-afternoon and her father hosted a regular poker game at his house with some old friends.

Claire knew they wouldn't disturb her. Nothing short of a nuclear explosion would wake her today, but she also knew her father would insist on cancelling. He had so few fun times lately she didn't want him to sacrifice the one thing he looked forward to all week. He'd already sacrificed so much of his life.

She pushed the lift button, trying to work out a solution with a brain shrouded in the heavy fog of fatigue.

'Claire! Hang on.'

The lift pinged and Claire got in, holding the doors open for Campbell.

'Are you OK? You look done in.'

'Too many sleepless nights.' She shrugged dismissively and then blushed when she realised she'd drawn attention to their night together.

'Me, too,' he agreed quietly.

Despite her tiredness, warmth suffused her body. He was so close! If she just shut her eyes and leaned a little, she could rest her head against his chest. His magnificent chest.

'Every time I close my eyes, I think of you and me and Friday night, and then I can't sleep.' His voice was soft and she yearned to fall into it.

Silence filled the space between them. Claire felt herself sway towards him. She despaired at how her body still responded to the pull of his, despite overwhelming exhaustion. So much for awkwardness!

The lift arrived at their floor and the doors opened. Saved by the bell! Wake up, Claire! Damn, this conversation was too hard to have when her energy reserves were at zero. It needed to take a different direction.

'Well, lucky you,' she quipped, striding from the lift. 'At least you've had a chance to get to bed. I've had about two hours' sleep in total. I was at the centre all weekend, delivering babies. I'd just done all the paperwork on my six a.m. delivery and was almost out the door when I was summoned.'

'No wonder you're almost out on your feet!'

'Three days off now. I'm going to sleep like the dead.' She half smiled and stumbled. He caught her arm and steadied her before she fell on her backside.

Campbell resisted the urge to pull her close. She smelt fantastic and the feel of her skin beneath his hands was glorious. They stood stock still while the hubbub of hospital life went on around them. She looked at him through sleep-hazed eyes, her lips parted, strands of her dark hair stuck to her lipstick.

'Can I do something for you?' he asked quietly, brushing the stray hairs from her mouth with one finger.

Yes. Pick me up and carry me away from here to a big nice soft bed somewhere and lie with me. Claire didn't know if lack of sleep was making her delirious, but suddenly a solution to her earlier problem was standing right in front of her.

'Do you mean that?' Some of the fog was clearing from her brain.

'Sure.'

'Are you? I know we didn't exactly part under the best of circumstances the other day…'

'I'm an adult, Claire. I can take it. What do you need?'

'A favour would be great.'

'Anything.'

'No strings?' This time she didn't want him to get the wrong idea.

'Of course!' His insulted look was rather endearing. 'Are you going to be at work all day?'

'Until about five.'

'Can I crash at your place?'

'Uh…sure.' Confusion furrowed his brow. 'Why? I mean, what's wrong with your place?'

'My dad has a poker game at our house every Monday morning. If I'm home, sleeping, he'll be stressing out about being quiet. I don't want to spoil his fun.'

'I knew I loved poker for a reason.' He grinned and fished his keys out of his pocket.

'It's just for five or six hours. I'll be gone by the time you get home.' She was suddenly serious. 'I will be gone, Campbell.'

'I know. I know.'

Claire let herself into Campbell's apartment and rang home straight away. She informed her father of her whereabouts and that she'd be home later in the afternoon. He seemed quite pleased by the arrangement. No doubt, all part of his push to have her get out more.

Zombie-like, Claire got in and out of the shower and quickly towelled herself dry on one of Campbell's fluffy towels. It was kind of bizarre, being here again after all that had happened between them.

She could have picked up the phone and dialled a handful of friends who would have been only too happy to oblige and give her a bed for the day. Why ask Campbell? The one person she should be keeping her distance from?

Because he'd been right there when the idea had come to her. He had been the quickest, easiest and most convenient person to ask. No wasting time, ringing around. Just a quick request and a quick answer. Tired minds didn't always come up with the wisest ideas!

Plus, geographically, his place was the closest. It hadn't even taken her ten minutes to get here. When bone-deep tiredness had you in its grip, a long car trip could end in disaster.

Claire briefly debated where to sleep. Campbell had a guest bedroom, she should use that. But as she stood in his doorway, his king-sized bed beckoned. The bed where she had slept with him only a few nights before. It was unmade, the sheets twisted, the pillows skew. She could almost picture him in it. Maybe if she'd been less tired and had had greater capacity to think rationally, she'd have chosen the guest room, but his bed was just too tempting to ignore.

As her head hit his pillow, she wondered fleetingly at the wisdom of being naked in his bed. But she was going to be out of here before he got home. Besides, she was too tired to move now. And the pillow smelt so-o-o good. It smelt like man. It smelt like Campbell.

                    *   *   *

For a day that had started out as bleakly as Campbell's, it had improved rapidly. Just the thought of Claire in his bed was enough to keep a smile permanently plastered on his face. Campbell's behaviour was enough, without gossip from William Casey, to confirm to all and sundry at St Jude's that he had indeed made progress with Sister West.

Campbell was sure he even saw money exchange hands on some of his rounds. It seemed his frivolity, along with the idiotic grin that he didn't seem to be able to shift, was enough to declare him the winner. Given that the opposite was true, he knew Claire would be furious, but he was just too damned happy to care at the moment.

He tried really hard all day not to fantasise about her asleep in his bed. And not to speculate about what she was wearing, because that led to images of a naked Claire and he really couldn't concentrate on his job. At all.

And he had to keep reminding himself that she had insisted she wasn't going to be there when he got home. Still, at least he could lie down where she'd been and smell her scent once again. It had started to fade from his sheets.

Campbell had a morning theatre list, which he whistled his way through. It was amazing he didn't accidentally incise something he wasn't supposed to, given how shot his concentration was. Luckily, they were procedures he could perform with his eyes closed.

The last op was a Caesarean for transverse foetal position. This scenario was a no-brainer for Campbell. Babies lying sideways across the uterus couldn't be born any other way. He tugged the wet and slippery baby from the safety of her mother's womb and was pleased to hear the little girl wail heartily at the intrusion.

He held the baby up over the top of the drape so her parents could grab a quick look before a nurse whisked her off to check her over. She returned the precious package to the parents a few minutes later, wrapped up as snug as a bug in a rug. Baby Anne looked very content, Campbell thought as he prepared to close the surgical incision.

He tried to tackle some paperwork at lunchtime but instead daydreamed about Claire and subsequently got nothing much achieved.

His afternoon clinic commenced at two and was filled with the usual antenatal checks. Weight, urine, baby's position, foetal growth and heartbeat.

He'd finished for the day and was signing his name to the last chart when Andrea popped her head in.

'Sorry, Campbell, I've just had a call from Hillary Beetson.'

'Do I know her?' Campbell searched his memory bank unsuccessfully.

'No. She's one of Martin's patients, but everyone has left for the day and you're on call. She's just rung to say she hasn't felt the baby move all day. I told her to come straight up and you could squeeze her in.' She ended with a sweet, pleading look, handing Hillary's chart to him.

'How many weeks?'

'Thirty-six.'

Despite Campbell's urge to make a quick getaway, he knew he had to see this client. 'Let me know when she gets here,' he sighed, thumbing through the chart.

The scenario was common enough. As the pregnancy reached its advanced stages and the foetus grew larger, there was less and less room for the baby to move. Decreased foetal movements were common in the last few weeks and usually meant nothing.

But Campbell also knew that it couldn't be ignored. An intra-uterine death at this late stage was unlikely but it was one of the more sinister possibilities. He pushed fantasies of Claire at home in his bed to one side and focused.

Five minutes later Andrea informed him that his patient had arrived.

'Afternoon, Hillary,' he greeted her confidently, introducing himself.

'Hi,' she said. She looked anxious and Campbell pulled up a chair beside his patient, hoping to allay her fears.

'Andrea tells me you haven't felt the baby move today.'

'That's right, I only realised a little while ago I haven't felt any movements since last night. It's usually so active but I've been so busy today…' she replied softly, obviously worried. 'What does that mean?'

'Nothing usually,' Campbell reassured her, 'there's not a whole lot of room for the baby to move around now, so it's common enough to go for longer than usual without feeling the baby move.'

'Oh. OK. That's a relief,' Hillary exhaled loudly.

'We'll just listen for the heartbeat first and then see if we can't prod it into giving us a kick.'

Hillary got up on the examination bed and Campbell waited while Andrea had squirted some gel on Hillary's bulging abdomen, running the Doppler through it to locate the heartbeat.

Campbell watched Andrea try several spots where the heartbeat was usually found. Nothing. Andrea stopped and palpated the abdomen, locating the baby's head low down in the pelvis, satisfying herself that she was indeed looking in the right places. Silence still greeted her attempts to find the heartbeat.

She turned to Campbell and handed him the transducer. Her eyes said it all. She was worried. Campbell felt the first prickles of impending doom.

'What's happening?' asked Hillary, the worried edge back in her voice. 'Why can't we hear it?'

'They can be tricky to find sometimes,' Campbell said, injecting into his voice a confidence he didn't feel.

He got Andrea to try and stimulate the baby to move while he ran the transducer all over, listening for the *whup, whup, whup* that indicated life. She poked and prodded. Nothing.

Campbell was very concerned now. 'Get someone from Ultrasound up here now,' he told Andrea, his voice calm but his eyes conveying urgency. She left immediately.

'What's wrong?' Hillary asked, raising herself on her elbows, tears gathering in her eyes. 'Why can't you find it?'

'Sometimes the baby's position can make it really hard. Sometimes the mother's heartbeat can confuse things. I want to get an ultrasound. We'll know more after that. It's probably just the baby playing hard to get.' He smiled, trying to reassure her. 'Why don't we ring your partner to come and be with you?'

'I rang Danny already. He should be here soon.'

Danny, Andrea and Darren from Ultrasound all arrived together a couple of minutes later. Campbell explained to Danny what was happening.

'What's the worst-case scenario, Doc?' asked Danny, coming right to the point.

'Let's just get this picture first. I don't want us to get ahead of ourselves.'

Andrea switched out the lights and Darren applied more gel to Hillary's tummy. Danny stood behind the bed, his hands on his wife's shoulders.

The screen flickered and their baby came into view. Darren manipulated the transducer to get a look at the heart. Campbell's worst fears were realised when no heart movement could be detected at all. He stared at the screen silently, willing the heart to move, to beat, but…nothing. The baby was dead.

Campbell felt an overwhelming, crushing sadness for this couple. He was going to have to give them news that would devastate them. Every part of him rebelled at having to be the one to do it. He ran his hands through his hair. Sometimes being a doctor really sucked.

He indicated to Andrea to turn the lights back on. 'Page the social worker,' he whispered to her as she passed him.

'Hillary, Danny,' he said, turning to them. 'I'm sorry to have to tell you this but we've just looked at your baby's heart and it's not beating. I'm sorry, but your baby has died.'

Hillary's face crumpled into a heap as she clutched at her husband's shirt. 'No, no, no,' she wailed. 'My baby, my baby.'

'What do you mean, dead? How can that be? What happened?' Danny demanded, his voice loud with anger and indignation.

'I don't know for sure,' said Campbell quietly. 'I'd like Darren to have a really good look and see if he can find the cause…if that's OK.'

'Do it,' said Danny, Hillary's sobs and cries of denial stimulating his aggression further.

Darren applied the transducer again and did a thorough ultrasound scan, looking for a reason for this tragic intra-uterine death. Hillary's sobs echoed around the room during the procedure.

Darren stopped and pushed a few buttons. 'There's no blood flow through the cord,' he said solemnly. 'There…' He pointed. 'I think that's the problem.'

'Is that a knot in the cord?' asked Campbell.

'I think so—it's kind of hard to tell. Might just be a lump

but, given that there's no flow, I'd say it's probably a true knot. The cord is quite long, which does increase the risk.'

Darren wiped Hillary's belly off and left the room. Andrea returned with Sharon, the social worker, and Campbell introduced her to the grieving couple.

'Did you find anything?' Danny asked, the angry edge to his voice dissipating as reality settled in.

'We think that there's a knot in the cord. We can't be certain until after the baby is born—'

'A knot? How can that happen?' Danny was angry again, his voice incredulous and demanding.

Campbell didn't take offence. The man had just had the rug pulled out from underneath him. Beneath Danny's veneer of aggression was a grief-stricken father. Campbell would feel the same way if it had been him.

'It's very rare but some babies can be so active that they can swim around in the womb and tie a knot in their cord. If it pulls tight enough, it can completely deprive the baby of nutrients from the placenta and they die.'

'I didn't think there was enough room at this stage for that,' said Danny.

'At this stage there isn't. It probably happened weeks ago, and the knot has been pulling tighter and tighter over the last few weeks as the baby grew more and there was less room to move.'

'Oh, God! I should have come in earlier,' sobbed Hillary. 'If only I hadn't been so busy… I should have been paying more attention.' Tears streamed down her face.

'It's not your fault, love,' Danny said gruffly, hugging her close, stroking her hair.

'He's right, Hillary. Cord knots are completely out of anyone's control. It was a freak accident. The baby probably died some time in the night. You did say the last time you felt it move was last night?'

'Yes, it was moving as I drifted off to sleep,' she sniffed.

'You weren't to know. Coming in earlier would have made no difference.'

Hillary's gut-wrenching sobs filled the room again and Campbell allowed them time to vent their grief. His skin puckered with goose-bumps as Hillary's wailing displayed her utter devastation. Campbell's heart went out to them. What did you say in this kind of a situation? He felt so helpless.

'What happens now?' asked Danny, wiping his tears and blowing his nose.

'We induce the pregnancy and Hillary will give birth to the baby. We don't have to rush into this. If you want time to think about everything, we could leave that till the morning.'

'Oh, God.' Hillary broke into loud sobs again.

'I'm so sorry, I wish I could have given you better news,' said Campbell, feeling wretched. 'I'm going to leave you now for a while and let you speak to our social worker. I'm going to be out at the desk if you need me for anything. I'll come and talk to you again after you've finished with Sharon.'

Campbell wandered to the nurses' station and sat down. His heart was heavy with the tragedy that had just unfolded. He'd give anything to not be here right now. To not have met this couple under these dreadful circumstances.

He'd have given anything to be at home with Claire. He needed her more now than he ever had. Just to feel the comfort and solace of her arms, to forget the awfulness of the day in the magic of her lips and the secrets of her body. To be held by the woman he loved.

Campbell used this time to write a thorough report in Hillary's notes. He documented everything from the beginning, including the ultrasound images that Darren had printed out for him. Such a waste, he thought as he signed the chart. So unfair!

'Campbell.' Sharon interrupted his thoughts.

'How are they?' Stupid question.

'No different from before. Devastated. They wanted me to ask you if you would perform a Caesar as soon as possible. Hillary doesn't want to be induced. She was booked for an elective Caesar with Martin anyway. I really think psychologically she wouldn't cope with waiting until the morning. She keeps saying she can't bear the thought of her baby being dead inside her. She wants to be able to hold it.'

'I'll go and talk to them. Thanks, Sharon.'

Campbell approached the room reluctantly. He didn't want to intrude on their grief. It was tragic enough for Hillary and Danny, without being forced to share such a personal time in their lives with people who were basically strangers. Even the intimacy of their grief wasn't sacred.

They looked up when Campbell entered. The soul-destroying cries had dissipated, replaced by expressions of utter disbelief and misery.

'Sharon said you'd like a C-section?'

Hillary nodded, her chin wobbling. 'She can't go through hours of labour to give birth to a dead baby, Doc. She just can't,' pleaded Danny.

'I can't do that, Campbell,' Hillary confirmed, tears coursing down her face.

'I understand,' Campbell reassured them gently. 'Are you sure you don't need more time? There really is no rush.'

'I want to be able to hold my baby,' Hillary cried. 'I don't want to wait. I want it to be over.'

'I'll arrange it immediately. I'll see you in Theatre in about half an hour.'

Andrea rang up to the operating rooms to check the emergency theatre wasn't in use, while Campbell made his way up there. He did so with a heavy heart. This would be no joyous event, like most Caesareans. There would be no lusty wail to bring a tear to the eye. Instead, he would have to pull out a stillborn baby. It was too sad for words.

The operation went without a hitch. Campbell felt profound sadness as he handed the lifeless baby boy to a waiting nurse. He knew they would wash the baby and dress him and have him ready to take to his parents when Hillary got out of Theatre. They would be able to hold their baby at last.

Removing the placenta was interesting as he was able to examine the cord close up. Sure enough, it was a true knot. He's never seen one in all the years he'd been in obstetrics.

Sometimes cords had a lumpy appearance, similar to a knot on a tree-trunk, but this one was a definite knot. He untied it to prove it to himself and so he could be one hundred per cent sure when he saw his client post-op.

Campbell finally got away from the hospital around nine o'clock. He'd stopped in and spent some time with Hillary and Danny. They were lying on the bed together, facing each other, their precious baby boy between them. They were crying and stroking his little face and talking to him as they held each other, and Campbell knew there was no easy way, no quick fix for their grief. They had a hard road ahead.

When Campbell pulled into his parking space he was surprised to find Claire's car still parked there. She was still here? He'd expected her to be long gone. He breathed a sigh of relief. After today he needed to hold her desperately.

Claire was dressing hurriedly when she heard Campbell's key in the lock. 'Oh, hell,' she cursed under her breath.

Why had she slept so long? Now she had no choice but to face him.

She looked at her attire, a pair of Campbell's baggy gym shorts turned over several times at the waist and pulled down low on her hips to anchor them. A flannelette shirt, also Campbell's, with the sleeves rolled up. Even her undies were a pair of Campbell's cotton clingy boxers.

It was either that or get back into her uniform. Yuck! She obviously hadn't thought about a change of clothes in her tired rush this morning.

'Campbell, I'm sorry, I know I'm still here,' gushed Claire, rushing into the lounge room, her attention on buttoning up the flannelette shirt. 'I'll get out of your hair straight away, I promise.'

Job complete, she turned her attention to him. She stopped in her tracks. Oh, lord, she thought, he looked awful. Her awkwardness at being caught still in his apartment and in his clothes diminished instantly.

'What's wrong?' she asked. 'What's happened?'

'Awful day.' He grimaced and ran his fingers through his hair, pushing his floppy fringe back. He walked past her and sat on the lounge, throwing his keys onto the coffee-table.

'How awful?' She sat beside him, not too close, sensing his need to vent his angst.

'I've just delivered a thirty-six-week stillborn baby boy. First true knot in a cord I've ever seen.'

'Oh, Campbell,' Claire gasped quietly, putting her arm around his shoulders. 'That's terrible.'

Claire listened while Campbell filled her in on the details. She absently rubbed his shoulder and caressed his forearm, her head pressed to his in shared sorrow.

'Sometimes I hate my job so much. I just felt so helpless, you know? Life is so bloody unfair.'

'I know,' she soothed quietly. She knew it well.

Campbell pressed his fingers to his temples and supported his face in his hands. Claire stayed silent, hoping her presence was some support.

They worked in a field that had its share of tragedies. Some got to you more than others. She'd been where Campbell was. She wouldn't desert him in his hour of need.

He raised his head and turned to look at her, giving her a small, sad smile that pulled at her heart. She smiled back, acutely aware of his maleness and his proximity. She felt the intensity of his gaze on her mouth and felt herself sway closer.

The sadness in his eyes drew her like a magnet. They called to her. She wanted to erase his pain and help him forget the last few hours. Every part of her knew she shouldn't, but he was hurting and he needed her.

His lips touched hers and she sighed into him. The potent need evident in his kiss forced a moan from deep inside her.

'I need you tonight, Claire. Don't leave.'

The rawness of his request as he cradled her face couldn't be denied. She knew what it felt like to need someone to seek solace in. She stood and followed him to his bedroom.

Their love-making was different this time. The frantic, desperate, bordering-on-obsessive need to mate had lessened. Campbell felt as if they were making love underwater. Slow and languorous, their touch unhurried. More explorative than explosive.

When he entered her she gasped his name and clutched him to her. He revelled in the feeling of connection. He wanted to stay inside her for ever. At least here, sheathed inside her, he finally felt close to her. In the world outside this bed, she never let him close enough.

He moved slowly inside her. She moaned and he felt her tighten around him. He pulled out a little and slowly re-entered. The slightest of movements, the most erotic pressure. Three more agonisingly slow pulses and Campbell could feel his orgasm build. At the same time Claire was raking her nails down his back as she spasmed around him.

The contractions of her climax pushed him over the brink. Then he collapsed on top of her, waiting until their breathing had settled before rolling onto his back.

They lay staring at the ceiling for a few moments. Claire felt her eyelids growing heavy again as post-coital malaise invaded her bones.

'Claire…'

'Shh,' she whispered, turning to rest her head against his shoulder. 'Don't talk. Just sleep.'

Claire woke a couple of hours later. She was alone. Alone with the realisation that she'd done it again. Slept with Campbell after she'd told him it wasn't going to happen.

But lying there with only her thoughts for company she could finally be honest with herself. She'd wanted it to happen. Friday night, last night and for many more nights. She was attracted to him, even more so now she'd seen his vulnerable side. She could fight it or she could run with it and finally have a bit of fun in her life.

She turned on her side, smoothing his pillow and wishing he were there beside her. Would he agree to be her lover? She couldn't do long term. Would he agree to that? One thing was for sure, there would be no misunderstandings this time. A relationship was possible on her terms only.

Her stomach grumbled and Claire realised she hadn't eaten in over twelve hours. She rose and groped around in the dark for something to wear. She found the light to the *en suite* and squinted at the insult to her pupils. A fluffy navy gown hung on a hook near the bath. She slipped into it and was immediately surrounded by soap and aftershave. Very manly.

Leaving the bedroom, Claire went in search of Campbell. They needed to talk and she was starving. She found him sipping a glass of wine on the balcony. A toasted sandwich was in the process of being devoured.

She reached over his shoulder and grabbed one of the cut portions. She sat down opposite him, devouring it instantly.

'Hello, sleepyhead.' He smiled.

'I'm so sorry I fell asleep, Campbell. I should have tried to stay awake. Some support I was!'

He pushed the plate towards her, offering her the last piece. She grabbed it before he could change his mind.

'You helped more than you can know.' Silence stretched between them. 'I'll make you another, shall I?'

'Yes, please.'

'Drink? Wine?'

'Coffee would be nice,' she said, swallowing the last bite.

He rose to go, the light from the lounge framing him. He was dressed in cotton boxers, similar to the ones he'd ripped off her earlier, that clung to his muscular thighs. His unbuttoned shirt flapped in the light breeze, revealing his hard stomach and smooth chest. He truly was magnificent.

Soon the aroma of brewing coffee and toasting bread intruded on Claire's thoughts. Her stomach growled in response and she was most grateful when he plonked a plate of toasted sandwiches in front of her. They ate in silence until the plate was empty.

'We need to talk,' he said, and she nodded.

'You first,' she invited.

'If tonight has taught me one thing, Claire, it's that life

is short. Whether you want to admit it or not, there's something between us that can't be ignored.' Campbell wanted to tell her he loved her, but couldn't bear to make his day worse should she reject him. 'I think we should explore it, see what happens.'

'I agree.'

'You do?' Campbell should have been ecstatic but he was suspicious. It was too easy. 'You mean you want to do more of this?' Campbell hardly dared to breathe lest she change her mind. He couldn't quite believe what he was hearing. She'd just done a complete about-face.

'Yes.' Claire smiled at Campbell's doubtful expression.

'Why the sudden change of heart?' Campbell needed to understand her motives. It still seemed too easy.

'Isn't it a woman's prerogative?'

'Apparently.'

Claire sighed. 'I don't know, Campbell. I only decided just now and I'm making it up as I go along. All I know is that you make me feel good and we're amazing in bed. And I don't want to give that up yet.'

'Yet? Does that mean that a time will come when you will give it up?'

'Yes.'

Campbell pushed back his chair and wandered over to the rail, gazing out over the river. He wanted for ever. Not just for now, or for as long as she wanted. Could he have the kind of relationship she was describing, waiting each day for the axe to fall?

'There's more,' she said, and he gripped the railing tight. 'Some ground rules. No L-word. No marriage proposals. No cohabitation.'

'What's left?' His voice held a bitter edge as he braced himself for her answer. Her cool dismissal of the things he wanted most wounded like barbs tearing his flesh.

'Sex and laughter and fun. Good times, Campbell. I don't know how long for. Let's just take each day as it comes. Oh…and another thing. You have to promise to let me go when the times comes.'

Claire felt dreadful, talking in such a detached manner. But she was trying to be honest. She had to lay her cards on the table now so he knew exactly where he stood. She didn't want to start this thing under false pretences. Well, not too many anyway.

She knew she couldn't have for ever with Campbell—she wouldn't inflict that on anyone. But being with him had been so amazing. As long as they kept their relationship in perspective as a temporary distraction, they could have amazing for a bit longer. Maybe a lot longer.

Campbell was torn. This was a man's dream come true. A relationship based entirely on sex and good times, with no fear of commitment. Before he'd met Claire, it was the kind of situation he would have jumped at.

Except now he wanted all the things she didn't. Could he promise to watch her walk away? To just let her go? Why was she so determined to avoid committing herself? Why? Why? Why?

'Why?' he spun around, facing her. 'Why the rules? What are you so afraid of?'

'Don't ask me why. I won't tell you. My reasons are my reasons. You're just going to have to accept that I have them.'

'Are they good?'

'Yes.'

He eyed her seriously. Claire could tell he was weighing up his options. His fringe flopped down in his eyes and the breeze lifted his shirt flaps aside, revealing tantalising glimpses of his firm torso.

Claire felt desperation invade her body. Now she'd made

up her mind she wanted him to agree very badly. His silence was making her nervous. Worse, she was convinced he was going to turn her down as each silent second dragged on. She had to do something to convince him. She'd never wanted anything this much.

'What do you say, Campbell?' Her voice trembled as she began to untie the belt of her robe, desperation making her bold. 'Do you want me? Want this?' she parted the robe until he could see her nakedness. 'Even if it's only for a little while? Or do we call it quits now?'

Campbell's hungry gaze devoured her body. His response was instantaneous and unable to be hidden in his clinging cotton boxers. He watched her triumphant smile, and he should have resented her for it but he wanted to take her so badly now he couldn't think straight.

He wanted to yank her up off the chair, push her against the bricks and have her against the wall. He wanted to teach her she shouldn't tease, and punish her for closing herself off to his love.

'Claire.' His voice was low and husky. 'That's not playing fair.'

'Say yes, Campbell. You know you want to.'

'You think you can sway me with your body. You think I can't resist you?'

She could see he was angry. He looked brooding and dangerous, and strangely enough it was really turning her on. Her breathing was ragged and her blood roared in her ears. 'Why do you even want to?'

He stalked over to her chair, pulling her up into his arms, grinding her against his straining erection. He was breathing heavily, his hooded eyes piercing her with rabid lust and intense dislike. She accepted the punishing force of his mouth on hers, matching his onslaught.

They pulled apart, chests heaving. Campbell yanked the

robe down and off her arms until she was completely naked in his arms. Their eyes locked in a silent battle of wills.

'Not fair,' he muttered with a brief bruising kiss. And then he picked her up. Striding into the lounge room, he threw her on the couch. He tore his clothes off, joining her on the narrow space, entering her immediately, his kiss silencing her cry of exultation.

He was so riled and so turned on it was hard to know where one emotion started and the other ended. He wanted to punish her for hurting him. He wanted her to feel his pain. He wanted to brand her so she belonged to him, despite what she thought.

Claire welcomed each thrust greedily. She lifted her hips to take him deeper, welcoming the pounding and cried his name as his mouth fastened roughly on her nipple. He sucked hard and grazed his teeth against it until she was ready to faint from the pleasure.

'Look at me!' he demanded.

Claire opened her eyes. Their gazes locked and held even as Campbell's increased pounding rocked her head back and forth. She bit her lip and cried his name as her release swamped her. She fought the natural urge to shut her eyes, wanting Campbell to witness her ecstasy.

Campbell's eyes widened at the wild abandon in hers. It was enough to take him right over the edge. He too fought the urge to close his eyes as his body shuddered and released inside her. He kept them open, sharing the tumult of his orgasm as she had shared hers.

CHAPTER SEVEN

IT SEEMED to take an age for their breathing to return to normal. Campbell lay spent and collapsed on top of Claire, silently berating himself for letting her goad him into such an ardent response. He pushed away, sitting up on the lounge, gathering his wits.

'You won't regret it,' Claire said breathlessly.

'I already do,' he said. Disgust filled his voice as he stalked over to where he had discarded his clothes and put on his underpants.

The smile slipped from her face. 'Campbell?'

'It's no good. I can't do it.' He retrieved his robe and threw it at her.

'Do what?' she asked quietly, catching the robe.

'Have a relationship with you on those terms.'

'What? Sex without commitment?' Claire laughed incredulously, belting the robe. 'Most men I know would jump at the chance.'

'I want more.' His voice was quiet but emphatic.

Claire could feel him slipping away. She'd obviously underestimated his moral fortitude. Now she'd made up her mind, she didn't want him to walk away, but it was important that she was clear with him.

'I'm sorry. I can't give you more.' She took a step towards him but he held up his hands and she stopped.

'I can't live by your stupid rules.'

'That's just your pride talking,' she stated, swallowing a lump.

'No. It's self-respect. You've led me a merry dance,

Claire, but enough is enough. We either agree to an equal relationship on mutual terms or...'

'Or what?' she asked quietly.

'We're finished.'

Campbell left the room and stood in the cool night air on the deck. He clutched the railing, begging the fates to make her see sense. He was taking a gamble. He knew that. But for the first time she'd admitted to wanting a relationship with him—but did she want it as badly as he did?

One thing was for sure, he wasn't going to let her toy with him any longer. Sure, being her plaything would, no doubt, be a thoroughly enjoyable and unforgettable experience, but he loved her and he needed her to give him more of an emotional investment. He'd rather lose her than be with her every day and not be able to tell her how he felt.

Anger and frustration and desperation chased around and around in his head and weighed heavily in his heart. What was taking her so long? The suspense was killing him. He was about to storm back inside and demand a response when he heard the front door open and then click shut. He had his answer.

Days came and went. Weeks passed. Claire hardly noticed. She felt as if she was living in a movie scene where the main character walked along obliviously as the scenery changed behind her, indicating the passage of time.

When she'd left Campbell's apartment that fateful night, it had been with the decision not to look back. Dwelling on what had been or could have been was a recipe for disaster. They'd had some good times. She chose to think of them instead of what she was missing.

Ten years ago, when her mother had been first diagnosed, it would have been easy to fall apart and wallow in self-pity, but she'd chosen not to, focusing on her career instead. She'd decided right from the outset that she wasn't going to let the disease define her, as her mother had done.

No way had she been going to sit around and wait for her genetic lottery ticket to come up. Life was there to be lived, so she'd lived it. She'd travelled and she'd back-packed and she'd nursed in remote locations and had steadily built a career to be proud of. Work had been her salvation. And so it was again.

Irritatingly, Claire found herself once more at the centre of St Jude's rumour mill. She weathered the curious looks and the whispered conversations with polite silence and years of practice, despite its outrageous content. Give the grapevine a juicy titbit and the details, no matter how fanciful, were made up as it went along.

Claire contemplated posting a memo on the notice-board in the foyer, stating that nothing had happened between her and Campbell and that they were only colleagues. Anything to stop the Chinese whispers.

It was difficult enough just being in the same hospital as Campbell. St Jude's was big, but it wasn't that big. Inevitably they ran into each other. At those times they behaved professionally, treating each other with politeness and respect. It was formal and a little strained, but it worked.

They were very careful not to get too close. In fact, Claire was aware of Campbell actually physically distancing himself when necessity required them to be closer than a safe distance. Claire knew she should, too, but was amazed at the degree of difficulty of such a simple task.

Just as hard was having to talk to him about a patient or a related matter while her mind was elsewhere. Like in bed with him naked and inside her. It was cold comfort but Claire knew she had done the right thing. The only thing.

He wanted long term and she could only give short term. As much as her body yearned for him, she was a time bomb he couldn't handle.

And then there was the gossip about all the dating he'd been doing. Apparently leopards didn't change their spots, and Campbell had returned to his old ways.

Claire didn't want to admit how much it hurt. After all, he was a free agent. Besides, she knew that listening to gossip or, worse, actually believing it was stupid. It had, no doubt, been blown completely out of proportion. However, the rumours persisted.

In an effort to scrub Claire from his mind, Campbell also threw himself into his work. Still, even one month on, it was difficult to forget when everywhere he went and everything he did at St Jude's reminded him of Claire.

His ultimatum and her subsequent rejection still felt like a raw, gaping wound. His mind kept on replaying it like an old movie projector stuck in a rut.

He was moody and distracted and even snappy on a couple of occasions. It wasn't anybody's fault but he was taking it out on whoever was unfortunate enough to cross his path. It was so unlike him yet he didn't seem to be able to stop.

His concentration was shot, particularly in the operating theatre, which made him annoyed. Consequently he was demanding and picky and ruining his status among the theatre staff who were already jaded from one too many prima donna surgeons.

Trying to distract himself with a bevy of beautiful, available women wasn't working either. His heart and mind really weren't in it, and that wasn't fair to them. He made up his mind to cease all such behaviour forthwith! There was only one woman he wanted.

He just hadn't bargained on how hard it would be to act normally around her. So hard, in fact, he avoided it like the plague. But when you worked in the same building and your professional lives crossed paths frequently, coming face to face was inevitable.

Campbell had to actually physically move back in her presence. She was too tempting when they were unavoidably thrown together. Her scent was so familiar to him, so addictive he had to suppress the urge to lean in and inhale along the curve of her neck where he knew she smelt the sweetest.

He missed that smell. It had dissipated quite quickly from his bed and his unit, and damn it all—he wanted it back!

A week later, Claire's phone rang and she picked it up. It was Casualty.

'Claire, we need you here. We have a patient of yours who's arriving in about two minutes in premature labour.'

'Who?' Claire heard alarm bells ringing in her head.

'Lex Craven.'

'She's twenty-eight weeks, isn't she?'

'That's right. I've already paged Campbell.'

'I'm coming now.'

Claire hurried down to Casualty, her mind running through all contingencies. The odds for premature babies had improved dramatically with modern drugs and supportive respiratory measures, but twenty-eight weeks…that was quite early. Where prematurity was concerned, the longer the gestation the better the baby's chances.

A lot was going to depend on the size of the baby and the maturity of its lungs. Hopefully it wouldn't come to that. They might be able to stop the labour if it wasn't too far advanced, or at least delay it a little to allow the administration of steroids to help mature the baby's lungs.

Claire was so focused on achieving a good outcome for Lex and her baby, the thought of having to work closely with Campbell was completely secondary. The most important thing was they put aside their awkwardness and act as a team. They were both professional enough for that.

She arrived slightly out of breath, adrenaline energising her blood in anticipation. The Casualty department was bedlam.

'Claire.' The nurse who emerged from behind the curtains of the obstetric cubicle greeted her, handing her a gown as she washed her hands. 'Campbell's just arrived. It's a madhouse here. There's an arrest in cubicle two and the neonatal team are dealing with an emergency in Theatre. They've been paged and will get here as soon as they can. It's just you and Campbell for the moment.' She gave a lewd wink and Claire rolled her eyes. 'The minute anyone becomes available I'll send them your way.' She scurried away, pushing a pole laden with pumps.

When Claire entered the cubicle, Campbell was hooking Lex up to the CTG machine to monitor the baby's heart rate. Lex was hysterical—crying, moaning and writhing around on the narrow trolley.

'I can't have the baby now,' she cried. 'It's too early. Please, please,' she begged them. 'I don't want my baby to die.'

Brian was trying his best to calm and comfort his wife, but Campbell's relief at seeing her was palpable and Claire didn't need to ask to assess what he needed first.

'Lex,' Claire said loudly, to cut through the woman's hysteria.

'Claire… Oh, Claire. My baby, please, my baby.' She burst into renewed tears.

'Lex.' Claire gripped her hand firmly. 'I know this is a worrying time for you, but it's very, very important that you calm down.'

'But my waters broke. I'm bleeding and it's too early,' she sobbed.

'I know, but we won't know anything for sure until we've checked you out. It's imperative you stay still so Campbell can assess how the baby's doing. Now, take some deep breaths and calm down. Come on,' she encouraged, demonstrating how she wanted it done. 'Breathe with me.'

Lex started to relax a little, which allowed Campbell to get a good trace of the baby's heart rate.

'One hundred,' he said quietly, but loud enough for Claire to hear. A little slow.

'Shall I get a speculum?' she volunteered, swapping the hand-holding job with Campbell.

'Lex,' he said, 'I need to check and see if you're dilated at all. Your membranes have ruptured so this baby obviously wants out, whether we like it or not. The only choice now is whether to let you deliver normally or to section you, and that will depend on your dilatation.'

'But it's too early for the baby to be here,' she sobbed.

'Obviously I wish the baby was further along, but the choice is no longer ours. Don't worry, Claire and I are here.' He shot a reassuring smile at Lex.

Claire handed him a speculum to allow him visual access to Lex's cervix. 'You want me to give her this?' she asked, holding up the empty ampoule of steroids she had already prepared in a syringe.

'You read my mind,' he said, his brow puckered in concentration as he removed the speculum and felt the amount of dilatation with his fingers. 'Fully dilated.' He grimaced as Claire injected the steroids into Lex's leg. This would hopefully have some effect on maturing the baby's lungs.

Ideally, two doses were given before the premmie baby was born, but they obviously weren't going to have enough time.

Lex groaned as a contraction swamped her body, and Claire noted the baby's heart dip into the sixties. She glanced at Campbell and his eyes mirrored her concern.

'Oh, no! I need to push!' Lex cried, alarm causing more tears to fall.

'Lex, you're fully dilated.' Campbell's calm voice took control of the situation. 'I want you to push, go with it. Push.'

Lex face reddened as she pushed down with all her might. When the contraction eased she said, 'What about a Caesarean?'

'Not enough time. This baby will be out quicker than I can section you. Now, I'm not going to lie to you. The baby does seem to be showing some signs of distress so the quicker you can push it out, the better.'

Lex started to cry again, working herself up very quickly. Claire had to get Lex to settle and focus if they were going to get the baby out quickly.

'Lex, we're here. Trust us. Stay calm and push on the next contraction.'

With Claire's soothing, Lex settled again and Claire encouraged her to channel her anxiety into the pushing. Five minutes later a tiny baby girl slid safely into Claire's waiting hands.

Thankfully another nurse arrived just at that moment to tend to Lex, which freed Claire to help Campbell resuscitate the small and as yet silent neonate.

'Doesn't look very big. Eight hundred grams if we're lucky,' Claire said in a low voice, placing the baby in the specialised resuscitation cot, complete with overhead warmer and removable sides for easy emergency access.

'She's barely breathing.' Adrenaline pounded through Claire's system as her trembling hands hooked the baby up to the monitor. 'Heart rate fifty.'

Claire's fingers worked rapidly administering gentle chest compressions as Campbell fitted a mask attached to a bag over the baby's face, enabling him to give respiratory support to the baby's feeble attempts at breathing.

'I'll need to intubate,' he stated, grabbing a thin curved plastic tube handed to him by a member of the neonatal team, who had burst through the curtain seconds ago.

Campbell felt adrenaline charge into his system, kicking his heart rate up and honing his concentration. His hand shook and he took a deep breath. He would not lose another baby.

Claire continued working as he quickly passed the tube down the baby's throat and into her lungs. Campbell exhaled the breath he'd been holding, but there was still too much to do to dwell on the success of the tricky procedure.

'Adrenaline,' he said, as he attached the breathing tube to the bag and puffed one hundred per cent oxygen into the little lungs.

Campbell quickly disconnected the bag again so adrenaline could be squirted down the breathing tube directly into the lungs. Claire watched the monitor as the heart rate accelerated to one hundred and eighty.

The collective sigh of relief could be heard outside the curtain as people started to relax, knowing that they had brought the tiny baby back from the brink. The first hurdle had been passed.

'Her lungs are very stiff,' Campbell commented to the neonatologist, who was dialling up settings on a portable ventilator. 'She'll need high pressure.'

Claire let the neonatal team take over and went back to

her patient who was inconsolable, desperately needing to know what was happening with her baby.

'Is she OK?' asked Brian.

'We've managed to secure her airway and get her heart to beat faster,' Claire confirmed cautiously.

'That's good, right?' asked Lex, an edge of hysteria in her voice.

Claire looked at Lex's and Brian's desperate faces, hungry for good news. She knew all they wanted was any scrap of positivity she could give them. It was a difficult line to walk. The compassionate nurse and human being in her wanted to help allay their fears and assure them everything would be OK.

But in reality she knew that the combined effects of their baby's prematurity, her weight and the high pressure needed to ventilate her were not good signs. As much as she wanted to, she couldn't give them false hope.

'She's over this initial hurdle. They're taking her to the neonatal intensive care unit. Her progress from now on will all depend on how her little lungs cope. Luckily, we have some very good drugs to help her in that department.'

'So she's not out of the woods yet,' Lex sniffed.

'No. In fact, she's quite critical.' Claire softened her voice to ease the blow. It had to be said. There was no point trying to put a positive spin on it when Claire knew the baby's chances were slim.

Lex began to cry again and Brian hugged her to him. Claire stood by silently, holding Lex's hand, giving them time to express their grief.

'But premmie babies do really well these days, right?' asked Brian. His face begged her to agree.

'Yes, some of them do really well,' she confirmed gently. Claire didn't have the heart to go into any more detail. She'd tried to prepare them for what the neonatologist

would say, but she didn't want them to give up all hope.
'Why don't we get you sorted and you can both go up and
see her?'

'Really? We'll be able to see her this soon?'

'Absolutely!'

Lex and Brian were cheered by this prospect and Claire
spent the next hour dealing with routine post-delivery matters. Campbell had gone to the NICU with the baby and
Claire was too busy to dwell on the heart-stopping events
that had just taken place.

Brian pushed his wife in a wheelchair to see their daughter, with Claire tagging along. On their arrival at the unit
they were put in a comfortable lounge area and told the
doctor would come and talk to them. Claire waited with
them—she couldn't leave them now.

Campbell found them there a few minutes later. Claire's
heart sank at the grim look on his face.

'Campbell.' Lex's voice lifted at his arrival, 'What's happening? Is she all right?'

'It's touch and go,' he said quietly, pulling up a chair to
sit close to them.

Lex's face crumpled and Campbell took her hand, rubbing it soothingly.

'The neonatologist will be here to speak to you soon. I
just thought you might like an update.'

'Claire said she's critical. Is that right?' Brian's voice
wobbled with emotion.

Campbell looked at Claire and smiled sadly at her worried face. He was glad she was there. Glad for Lex and
Brian, who were going to need a lot of emotional support,
and glad for him, too. Her presence helped make his words
easier to say. Knowing she was there to support him as
well as them was comforting. Giving people bad news was

never easy. Having someone you knew and trusted by your side was a godsend.

'Yes, Brian. Your baby is critical. She's needing one hundred per cent oxygen and special drugs to support her blood pressure. Her lungs are very hard to ventilate, they're very stiff. The machine that is breathing for her has to deliver her breaths under great pressure to even get them into her lungs. I won't lie to you. Her outlook isn't good.'

Claire closed her eyes, feeling dreadful for Lex and Brian and thankful that she didn't have to deliver such devastating news herself. She looked at Campbell. His face was as grim as the news he'd just imparted.

She felt a tug in the region of her heart. He hadn't had a very good run. He'd worked wonders today under great pressure but she wondered if he felt a sense of *déjà vu*. Having witnessed at first hand how affected he had been by Hillary's baby only weeks ago, she worried how he'd be if he lost this baby, too.

'What are her odds?' Brian asked gruffly.

'We'll be doing everything in our power to get her through this, Brian. But she's nearly on maximum support now so I'd say her chances are quite slim. I don't like to give percentages, the neonatologist will probably go through that with you, but she's so tiny. That's her biggest disadvantage at the moment.'

'How tiny?' asked Lex, realising that she knew almost nothing about her little girl—not even how much she weighed.

'Eight hundred and fifty grams.'

Claire's heart went out to Campbell as his words sank heavily into the silence that followed. No further words were necessary to impart the seriousness of her size. One thousand grams was the magic number for premmie babies. Those weighing less often didn't have good outcomes.

How could a baby so small ever survive? Even with the medical technology they had today? It would be a miracle. But, Claire reminded herself, miracles can and did occur in intensive care units all the time.

'Maybe we should think about getting her christened,' Brian said quietly to his wife, tears glistening in his eyes. Lex's shoulders shrugged up and down as she sobbed into her husband's shoulder.

Claire and Campbell sat in silence while the couple's grief echoed around the room. Claire felt helpless. What could you say to make things better? Nothing. All she could do was be there for them.

'Would you say a prayer with us, Campbell? Claire?' asked Brian quietly, lifting his head.

Campbell wasn't a religious man but he knew that people's faith could help them through extremely traumatic situations. Who was he to argue with that? Whatever helped Lex and Brian cope was worth a try.

They all joined hands and bowed their heads.

Claire was conscious of Campbell's hand engulfing hers and of their shoulders rubbing lightly together. The circle was intense and intimate and she felt a connection with Campbell she hadn't felt before. It suddenly seemed right to be here by his side.

Claire felt her heart thudding in her chest as a realisation began to dawn. This feeling of intensity and connection—she knew what it was. It was love.

Suddenly it was clear. She'd been in love with him all along and hadn't known it. Claire suppressed a groan. What a completely inappropriate time to have such an epiphany!

'Amen,' whispered Brian.

Amen, thought Claire.

A nurse entering the room broke the mood and startled Claire out of her introspection.

'I'm sorry we've taken so long to get to you, Mr and Mrs Craven. My name's Leah. I'm looking after your baby today. Julie MacDonald, the neonatologist, will speak to you both shortly. Would you like to come and see your daughter first?'

Leah spoke to the new parents on the way to the bedside about all the machines and tubes and monitors they would be seeing. She knew it was often devastating for parents to see their intensely monitored baby for the first time.

Claire and Campbell tagged behind slightly. It was hard for Claire to concentrate now. She was trying to come to grips with her revelation and act normally at the same time. A difficult thing to do when the man in question was so close she could feel the heat radiating from his body.

'She's so tiny,' Lex whispered, a tear running down her face as they watched the fragile little girl through the clear plastic of the isolette. Tubes and lines crisscrossed her practically transparent body. There didn't seem to be an area of skin that had escaped being covered by one thing or another.

'What's her name?' Claire enquired.

'Charlotte. After Charlotte Brontë. *Jane Eyre* is my favourite book,' replied Lex, her voice flat, her hand pressed to the plastic.

'It's a beautiful name,' said Claire, squeezing Lex's shoulder.

Julie MacDonald arrived and Claire withdrew, knowing that Lex and Brian were in good hands. She gave assurances she'd call back later when the new parents had digested some of the information. Claire arranged with Leah to page her should the baby's condition change for the worse.

Now all the drama was over Claire needed to be alone.

She had to get away from Campbell's presence to think. A lot had happened today. Professionally and personally.

Her hands trembled as she walked back to the birth centre. What kind of a fool had she been? She'd honestly thought she could deny love from her life. She'd thought that if she didn't allow a man into her life and didn't allow herself to think about it, or talk about it then it couldn't possibly happen. She'd been wrong. Love didn't work like that. You didn't get to choose where love was concerned.

She realised now that those feelings and emotions that had puzzled her so much after she'd met him, the ones she'd never experienced before, had been the first stirrings of her love for him. Her feelings for Shane had been puppy love in comparison.

She sat at her desk and cradled her head in her hands. Watching Campbell in action today, his compassion and gentleness with Lex and Brian, the way he'd empathised with them—that had done it. That had been the clincher.

She'd already witnessed his brilliant professional skills in highly stressful situations. She knew he was an excellent practitioner. But to see him connect and take the time to be with grieving people—that was special.

His involvement with Hillary and Danny and their baby was a perfect example. He cared. He got involved. Too many doctors departed after bad news and left it to the nurse to do the comforting. Not Campbell, and, heaven help her, she loved him for it.

Claire groaned and gave herself a mental shake. She swivelled in her chair so she could look out the window. It didn't matter anyway. That she loved him was immaterial. The facts of her life were still the same. Nothing could come of it.

So she'd just have to get over it. Yes, it was going to take time, but she'd acknowledged it, hadn't she? Surely that was the first step. She couldn't be with him, so pining was pointless. Besides, she never pined. Never. She got on with life. She did that really well.

Claire rose and wandered into the staffroom to get a cup of coffee, still not quite believing these strange new feelings. She should be happy—wasn't that how women in love felt? But it was hard to be excited about unwanted feelings.

OK, she loved him and, short of leaving St Jude's she was going to see a lot of him. So she had to sort out a way to handle it. They had to work together and they had to find a way to get back to their previous ease. This stiff formality since their split was awful.

Today they had worked together like old times. They had worked as a team for Charlotte. All their baggage had been left outside the curtain and they'd got on with the job.

She shouldn't be surprised. Their recent history not withstanding, he'd always been a pleasure to work with. He treated her as an equal, he was polite, funny, considerate and willing to listen and integrate her opinions and ideas. Claire realised suddenly she missed that dynamic.

It had disintegrated of late, replaced with awkwardness and formality. OK, she'd have to keep her love a secret, but she could do that if it meant they could return to their old professional relationship. If they couldn't be lovers, maybe they could be friends? Surely they were grown-up enough for that?

A knock on her door brought her out of her reverie. She glanced up. It was Campbell. Looking at him standing in her doorway, Claire marvelled at how it had taken her so long to get it. Her love was so obvious to her now.

She noticed his strained demeanour was back in place.

'Just checking in to see if you were OK…you know, after everything that happened today?'

Claire was touched by his consideration, even if it was

a little stiff. This was why she loved him. He cared and he was thoughtful.

'I'm fine.' She smiled, her voice husky. 'A little shaky still…'

'Yes…me, too,' he admitted, and gave her a ghost of a smile in return.

'Any update on Charlotte?'

'No. Still not looking good. They haven't been able to wind any of her ventilation back.'

He sounded so civil Claire could bear it no longer. She rose and took some steps towards him, but stopped when she saw him straighten and take a step back.

'Look, Campbell, I know this past month has been difficult…but we're both adults. I miss our professional relationship—the way it used to be. The way it was today. Can't we put what happened behind us and just be friends?'

She held her breath. All of a sudden she needed this more than anything. Maybe his friendship would be the perfect antidote for her love?

He regarded her seriously. Was the woman mad?

'Friends? Claire, I don't know if I could ever just be your friend.'

'OK. Maybe we can't be bosom buddies, but surely we can be friendly at least?'

'I think for some men and women, especially ones with history, being friends is…difficult.'

'But why, Campbell? Why does it have to be that way?' She took a couple steps closer, beseeching him.

'Because.' He pushed his floppy fringe out of his eyes impatiently. Hell! Was he going to have to spell it out?

'Because why?' Desperation tinged her voice. It would be such a relief to put their awkwardness behind them.

Obviously he was going to *have* to spell it out. 'Because whenever I see you I want to make love to you,' he said, trying to keep the exasperation from his voice. Was she that clueless?

The admission seemed to be wrenched from deep within him and Claire figured it hadn't been an easy thing to admit. She swallowed convulsively, his words melting her insides and calling to her love. It rose in her and threatened to spill out. No! She must stay focused.

'I know it'll be…strange at first, but it'll soon seem more natural. We just need a bit of practice. I'm tired of us being tense around each other. Everyone notices, you know. The gossipmongers are having a field day. If people can see that we're fine with each other, they'll leave us alone and gossip about something else instead. Aren't you sick of the speculation?'

'Yes,' he agreed wearily, rubbing his eyes. The scrutiny was a little wearying. To be able to act normally would be a nice change—or as near normal as was possible for ex-lovers. 'OK,' he conceded. 'I'd be willing to give it a go if you are.'

'Good. Oh, that's great. Thanks, Campbell. I feel so relieved,' Claire prattled, desperately wanting to go and hug him but rooted to the spot. A little too early in their friendship for that.

Campbell shook his head as he made his way back to his office. Friends? It was never going to work. How could he have a platonic relationship with the woman he loved? Every time he saw her he wanted to push her against a wall and have his way with her!

Her professionalism at the birth and resuscitation of Charlotte and her continued empathy, compassion and unspoken support of him today had only served to deepen his love.

Something told him he was going to suck at being friends.

CHAPTER EIGHT

A WEEK later Campbell had to concede that maybe he'd been wrong. The birth centre had been very busy all week, which had necessitated a lot of contact with Claire. Their pact to be friendly seemed to be working. They were both more relaxed and their professional relationship seemed to be getting back on track.

Of course, he was still as horny as hell at the very sight or smell of her, but as far as he knew no one had ever died from it and her friendly, easier way with him compensated to a degree. And then, of course, there were always cold showers. Campbell had never been cleaner in his life!

He whistled as he made his way over to the centre to check on a client who had delivered in the night. Claire was on day shift so he was bound to run into her. Maybe if he didn't push it, friendship could blossom into something more?

Claire was beaming when she bumped into Campbell.

'You look as if you've won a million dollars.'

'Better.' She grinned. 'Sometimes, Campbell, I love this job so much I just want to burst with it. You know?'

'Sure.' Campbell kept his smile in place and tried not to flinch at the ease with which she used the word 'love'. So it wasn't that she couldn't say it—she'd just never associated it with him. 'What happened?' he asked, following Claire to her desk.

'I helped your client with a breastfeeding issue. It never ceases to amaze me that human beings are born with the ability to bear young and then nurture them. I love watching mothers feeding their babies. It's truly wonderful.'

'Yep. It's a beautiful thing,' he agreed quietly. Images of Claire with a baby at her breast rocked him. His baby.

Friends. Friends. Just friends, he chanted to himself. Yep! Sucking at the being friends thing!

Oblivious to his inner turmoil, Claire stood to retrieve a file. A wave of dizziness hit her and she grabbed hold of the desk for fear she would faint. Nausea rolled through her gut. She sat down again quickly.

'Claire? Claire, are you OK? You're as white as a sheet.' He crouched beside her chair.

'I'm fine… I just feel a little light-headed,' she admitted in a small voice, fanning herself as a surge of heat washed over her.

'You don't look fine,' he said gruffly, grabbing her legs and dumping them up onto her desk.

'I'm sure it's just because I haven't eaten anything since breakfast,' she replied shakily, some vigour returning to her voice as she felt the blood rush back to her head.

'I'll get you a glass of cordial,' he said, leaving her side briefly before returning.

'Thanks.' She smiled gratefully. She reached for the water with a shaky hand, feeling the cool glass against the pads of her fingers before it slipped and smashed to the floor at his feet.

Claire sat up in horror, watching vacantly as the water pooled around their shoes. How clumsy!

Barbara bustled in to investigate the sound of breaking glass. 'Not again, Claire,' she tutted, after checking that Claire was OK. 'That's two glasses in as many days! You've been a bit of a butterfingers lately,' she teased, helping Campbell mop up the water.

'No, I'm not,' Claire denied absently, her thoughts still foggy.

'Oh, yeah? What about that tray of instruments you dropped in Theatre the other day during that Caesarean? Goodness, forgetful as well. Anyone would think you were pregnant,' she quipped, as she left the room with a soaked towel.

Claire stilled as she felt the beginnings of fear settle in her stomach. Pregnant...or worse. Barbara was right, she had been a bit absent-minded of late. She could feel herself tremble and a wave of nausea assailed her again. Clumsy as well. Oh, God. Please, no.

'Claire? Hey, Claire! What's wrong? You look terrible. She was only joking about the pregnant thing.'

Campbell was shaking her gently by the upper arms. She couldn't move. Couldn't speak. Fear paralysed her and kept her mute.

'I'm going to be sick,' she whispered, finally managing to speak and move her legs. She dashed to the toilet, her hand clamped over her mouth.

She retched and retched. Once the nausea had passed, Claire pulled the toilet lid down and sat. She was pale and shaken.

'Claire? Are you all right?'

Claire heard the concerned note in Campbell's otherwise gruff voice.

'I'm...I'm fine,' she answered, standing on wooden legs and flushing the toilet.

Campbell helped her out, assessing her pallor.

'I'm fine.' She raised her hand to fend him off and smiled weakly. 'I'll just throw some water on my face and I'll feel better.'

He watched as she splashed water on her face and neck. He handed her a towel.

'Better?' he asked gently, brushing her damp fringe with his long finger.

Claire nodded and allowed him to pull her close. She sank against him gratefully, ignoring the guilt she felt at breaching their new pact of friendship. She longed to stay in his embrace but knew it wasn't healthy for either of them. She broke away and walked on wobbly legs back to her desk.

She sat down, thankful that her head had now stopped spinning. Unfortunately, her mind had taken over. Was it possible that the first symptoms of her mother's disease, one she had a fifty per cent chance of inheriting, were emerging?

Clumsiness and forgetfulness. The hallmarks of Huntington's. Claire tried to keep the panic at bay and think logically. Was it possible to have had these symptoms for long and not realised it?

Ever since her split with Campbell she'd kept herself busy with her work in an attempt to ignore the emotional fallout. Nothing had mattered but her career and the birth centre.

She dismissed the possibility of pregnancy out of hand. They'd used contraception, it wasn't possible. For goodness' sake, they'd only had sex a few times! Although it was slightly preferable to the alternative, Claire had to admit that neither of them were great choices.

'I'll get you something to eat.' Campbell interrupted her swirling thoughts. His pager beeped and he pulled it impatiently off his belt.

'It's OK, Campbell. You go.' Claire assured him. She needed time to think without him being right there in front of her. She'd never been more scared in all her life and she didn't want that to be the catalyst to confess all to

Campbell. 'I'll sit for a bit and then I'll ask Barbara to get me something to eat.'

He hesitated. His pager beeped again.

'I mean it,' she insisted. 'I feel much better now.'

'I'm going to ring you later to check on you,' he threatened lightly.

She smiled weakly and watched him walk away, a sense of foreboding sitting like a lead weight in her stomach.

The week went from bad to worse. Not only did Claire have to contend with the growing fear that she had inherited her mother's disease, but the mere thought of it made her physically ill. Every time she thought about it, and that was practically always, she had to rush to the toilet. Nausea and vomiting were now her constant companions.

She tried hard to remember if her mother had suffered from nausea when she'd first become symptomatic. If she had, Claire couldn't recall it and Mary was in no position to confirm or deny it. She could ask her father, but there was no need to alarm him yet.

What she wouldn't give to have Campbell with her now. To be able to lean on him, tell him everything. The whole sorry story, including her love. Maybe things wouldn't be so scary and uncertain with him by her side.

A few days later she was sitting at her desk, trying to concentrate on the water-birth protocols she'd begun shortly after her break-up with Campbell. It had seemed like a good idea at the time, partly because she really wanted to see it come to fruition but mostly because she knew it'd occupy a lot of time. But try as she may, they just couldn't hold her attention today.

She was staring blankly, her mind going over and over the same things that had been fermenting there for days now. When her eyes refocused she realised she was staring at a big red ring around one of the dates on her desk calendar.

That was the day her period had been due. Tuesday the twelfth. Weeks ago! She was as regular as clockwork every twenty-eight days. Never missed. She sat up straighter.

She counted back and double-checked. How could she have not realised that she'd missed a period? OK, so she'd deliberately shut out everything other than work and her responsibilities at home but this was ridiculous.

It was probably nothing to worry about. To say she'd been under a lot of stress recently was a gross understatement. Just because nothing had ever affected her cycle before, it didn't mean that it couldn't. Trying to come to grips with a potential terminal illness would certainly do it!

The next morning, Claire had to admit that being pregnant was a real possibility. She'd risen early as usual to assist with her mother's care, and had to make a detour to the toilet before she could begin anything.

She felt a brief lifting of her spirits at the thought that the nausea might be related to pregnancy and not the disease. But that didn't account for her forgetfulness and clumsiness. Although most pregnant women she knew did complain of poor memory. So maybe...

As Claire parked her car at St Jude's a few hours later, she knew she had to find out.

'Barbara, I need you to take some blood from me.'

'OK. Sure. Everything OK?'

'No, not really. I think you were right. I might be pregnant after all.'

Claire was most grateful to Barbara who sympathised but didn't pry. She felt absurdly close to tears as Barbara assured her that the secret was safe with her.

The needle stung as Barbara slid it easily into the vein

at the crook of Claire's elbow. The syringe filled with dark red blood. She took off five mils and handed it to Claire.

'Thanks.' Claire plunged the needle into the top of a vacuum-sealed blood tube and watched as the blood was sucked from the syringe into the tube.

Barbara filled out the slip for the lab, writing 'Beta HCG' in the test-required box.

Beta HCG, the pregnancy hormone, responsible for the entire gamut of symptoms described by pregnant women the world over. It became detectable in the blood and urine at a very early stage.

To complete the form she needed to fill in the requesting doctor box. Barbara hesitated over this one. She pursed her lips and firmly put down Campbell's name, hoping that she'd done the right thing. She placed the blood sample and the form in a path bag and sent them off to the lab.

Thankfully Claire had a busy day of appointments and meetings. It wasn't until just before she was due to go home that she could check the computer for her results.

It took a few minutes to get into the screen she required. And there it was, blinking in bright green. POSITIVE.

Everyone had gone off for the day so Claire felt no embarrassment as she burst into tears. Life just wasn't fair. As if it wasn't bad enough that she'd convinced herself she'd inherited Huntington's disease. Now, apparently, she was pregnant. Her two worst nightmares had just come true.

How Claire got through the next few days, she really couldn't recall afterwards. She was pregnant. Pregnant with Campbell's child. And also, whether she wanted to face it or not, she had to confront the very real possibility of having Huntington's. A disease she could pass on to her baby.

A baby. Something Claire had always wanted, more than she could have articulated. Something she had known she could never have. But she was having one now, and she could think of nothing else.

Mercifully Campbell was away at the moment, attending a three-day conference in Melbourne. Not seeing him had given her the space she needed to look at their situation clearly.

She probably had Huntington's disease. Worse, she was pregnant with a baby that could also have the same illness. His beliefs about genetic disorders still rang in her ears, and her belief that she couldn't burden someone she loved with a potential invalid still stood. It was more important than ever that she keep her distance.

Claire kept turning over and over in her mind what she was going to do. All she really wanted to do was revel in the life growing inside her and daydream about happily-ever-afters. But there were decisions to be made.

How could she bring a child into the world with her family history? She'd hardly be protecting it if, by giving birth to it, she was exposing it to the same awful genetic lottery that she'd lived with for too many years.

At least Claire had had twenty carefree years before the axe had fallen. This little one would live every day of its life under a cloud. Sure, plenty of children lived under worse uncertainties, but this was her child. Claire knew she wasn't capable of giving her baby life knowing she could also be passing on a death sentence.

But was she? She had never been tested. There hadn't even been a test available when her mother had first been diagnosed, and after extensive genetic counselling, she'd decided not to bother. Not knowing was preferable to being told you were positive. As she had told Campbell, ignorance was bliss.

But she could no longer just think of herself. If she had the disease, her baby had a fifty per cent chance of inheriting it as well. Was that something she wanted to inflict on her baby? How could she live with herself if she'd passed it on?

Claire knew she was going to have to have the predictive test that had become available in the last few years. But knowing it and liking it were two different things.

Thinking positively helped. If she took the test and it was negative, then her and the baby were going to be OK and she could allow herself to love Campbell—if he still wanted her after all she'd put him through. Yes, she had to focus on love. Love for her baby and love for Campbell. It would get her through what had to be done.

She'd never been more terrified in her life!

The next day Campbell caught a taxi to St Jude's straight from the airport. He wanted to tackle the mountain of paperwork that would be waiting for him and, if he was honest, he wanted to see Claire.

He'd really missed her the last few days. OK, so their relationship wasn't exactly what he wanted, but they seemed to be moving into a comfortable friendship and he was surprised how much he'd missed that.

He removed his jacket and sat at his desk, pulling his bulging intray towards him. He opened the yellow internal mail envelope on the top of the pile and several lab forms fell out. He thumbed through them distractedly.

Campbell always insisted on looking at his own results. It was a double-check system that occasionally picked up abnormalities that had been missed or not reported to him, usually through communication breakdowns and human fallibility.

Nothing seemed out of the ordinary. Just the usual hotchpotch of pregnancy tests, blood counts and electrolyte studies. The last one was a pregnancy test. It was fairly unremarkable in itself, except for the name. Claire West. He sat perfectly still for a few seconds. Surely not? Claire? His Claire?

His heart started to beat a little faster. He looked at the date. It had been done four days ago. He took a deep breath to calm his suddenly raging thoughts. Could it be her? Her name was fairly common. There were probably hundreds of Claire Wests in Brisbane. There was no patient identification number either. Intriguing.

His hand shook as he dialled the number for the lab. He needed to investigate fully before he jumped to any conclusions. He rang off a few minutes later, having ascertained that the blood bearing Claire's name on that day had been logged as having come from the birth centre.

Pregnancy tests weren't usually sent from the centre. There was no need to perform one as the clients were obviously pregnant or they wouldn't have been cleared to attend.

Campbell felt a tremor slither through him. Claire was pregnant. She was going to have his baby. He stood up, trying to quell his growing excitement. Suddenly he wanted to jump for joy. He snatched the pathology form and shoved it into his jacket pocket. If he hurried he might catch her before she left for the day.

He had to see her and reassure her that everything would be OK. He'd be there for her and his child. She could stop running away from relationships. Whatever it was, they could work it out for the sake of the baby. They'd get married and live happily ever after.

Valerie informed him she'd just left and if he hurried he might catch her in the car park. He didn't need telling twice and he rushed out of St Jude's as fast as he could.

Campbell spotted Claire's head disappearing into her car as he arrived at the staff car park. He yelled out but she didn't hear. He bolted to his own car, deciding to follow her until she stopped and got out.

Traffic was always heavy at this time of the afternoon in and around the hospital, and Campbell found himself four or five cars behind. As they travelled further into suburbia, the cars thinned out and he was directly behind her for the last five minutes of the journey.

He drummed his fingers impatiently on the steering-wheel, waiting for her to look in her rear-view mirror so he could alert her to his presence. She must have been deep in thought as she never looked once.

She drove into a driveway in a pleasant suburban street. He parked out front and was undoing his seat belt when his mobile phone rang. He wanted to switch it off but answered it anyway. It was one of the midwives in Labour Ward, ringing about a private patient.

It took ten minutes to deal with the problem. He hung up eagerly and was knocking on Claire's front door in a matter of seconds.

A tall, grey-haired man answered. Campbell assumed him to be Claire's father and was struck by how old and tired he looked. Claire had told him he was sixty-four, but Campbell would have put his age somewhere in the seventies.

'Hello. Mr West? I'm Campbell Deane.' He held out his hand and the older man shook it. Campbell was surprised by the strength of his grip.

'So you're Campbell,' he said in a voice as firm as his handshake. 'I'm Ray, Ray West. Pleased to meet you.'

Ray ushered Campbell into the lounge. 'Is Claire expecting you?'

Campbell could tell that Ray was unused to meeting any of Claire's men friends. 'No.'

'I don't mean to pry, Dr Deane, but Claire did say you

weren't seeing each other any more. I don't know if she'll be too keen to see you.'

'Tell her it's important. Please.'

Ray left to talk to Claire while Campbell waited. He returned quickly.

'I'm sorry, Dr Deane. She doesn't want to see you. I'm afraid my daughter does have a rather large stubborn streak.'

'Yes, I'm well acquainted with that streak. Please, call me Campbell.'

'Well, Campbell, I think it's high time somebody came along and made her see that isolating herself from life isn't the answer. I admire your persistence.'

'Thank you. I fear I'm not out of the woods yet.' Campbell smiled.

He felt the older man's scrutiny and sensed Ray was trying to get his measure.

'Well, that's why I'm off to get the paper. That's a good long walk, about an hour. I expect you to use that time well. She's in the end bedroom.'

Campbell shut his eyes, unable to believe his good luck. Claire's father was on his side. He was grateful to Ray for his support—he needed as much as he could get.

Still, he approached the end door with a degree of trepidation. What he did and said now could make all the difference. Campbell felt the gravity of the situation weighing him down.

He raised his hand to knock and then hesitated. If he gave her the option, she'd no doubt deny him entry. She might even lock the door. He needed to speak to her face to face. Best not to alert her. Forewarned was, after all, forearmed.

He pushed the door open. Claire was in the middle of hanging a feedbag, winding it through a pump. It was obvious she hadn't been expecting him. Her expression went from startled to surprised and then, as her father's betrayal sank in, angry.

Campbell wasn't prepared for what he saw in the room. He stopped short, taking in the sight of Claire and the frail older woman in the bed. What was going on here? He didn't seem to be able to process his visual signals. Who was the woman? Was this her mother?

Claire cursed her father silently. She didn't want Campbell here. Now he was going to ask a whole host of questions she didn't want to answer just yet. She'd wanted to keep her mother's condition a secret, at least until after the test.

'Do, please, come in.'

Campbell didn't miss the anger, thinly veiled by sarcasm. 'I'm sorry, Claire…I didn't realise. Your father said you were in here. I assumed it was your bedroom.'

'I told Dad I didn't want to see you.'

'Yes, he told me. Then he went out to get the paper and told me where you were. I think he approves of me.'

Campbell's gaze returned to the occupant of the bed. She looked very frail, her papery skin stretched taut over her bones. She lay staring blankly into space. Campbell noticed drool pooling at the corner of her mouth.

It had to be Claire's mother. Despite the ravages of an obviously debilitating disease, the likeness was striking. Campbell's professional guess was a terminal illness of some kind. Probably cancer.

'Aren't you going to introduce me?'

'Campbell Deane, this is my mother, Mary West.'

'Pleased to meet you, Mrs West.' Campbell raised his voice slightly.

Mary didn't move. She didn't blink or acknowledge his

presence in any way. She continued to stare blankly at nothing in particular.

'I need to talk to you, Claire.' Campbell's request was gentle. He saw her mouth thin and knew she was still angry with him.

Claire finished hanging the feed set and turned on the pump. 'I'm going outside for a while, Mum.' She stroked her mother's hair as she spoke. 'I'm going to talk to Campbell, I'll be back shortly. We haven't read the paper yet.' Claire pressed a kiss against her mother's forehead.

Campbell followed her out of the room and into the lounge. She walked to the window, keeping her back to him.

'How long has she got?' Campbell watched as she stiffened slightly then sighed and pressed her forehead to the glass.

'The GP thinks months.'

'Oh, Claire, I'm so sorry.' He went to her and put his arms around her, pulling her into him. 'All this time you've been dealing with your mum's illness alone. Why didn't you tell me? Everything's so much clearer now. I've been making these demands...and all the time your mum's been dying.'

'My mother has nothing to do with our break-up. No, actually, that's not true. She has everything to do with it, just not the way you think.'

Campbell tried not to feel dismay at the flatness in her voice. He put his hand in his jacket pocket, desperately searching for a way to reach her. His fingers came into contact with the crumpled piece of paper he had hastily shoved there earlier. It felt like a message coming from his unborn child.

He handed her the lab report. She took it and read it without blinking.

'You're pregnant.'

'Yes.'

'With my baby.'

'Yes.'

Campbell wanted to swing her up in his arms and whoop for joy. 'What are we going to do about it?'

'*We're* going to do nothing. I haven't made up my mind yet. There are some…things I need to clarify first.'

Campbell heard the don't-mess-with-me edge to her voice. 'Don't you want the baby?' He tried not to sound as disbelieving and desperate as he felt.

Claire shut her eyes, wishing it were that simple. Tears suddenly threatened. She loved him so much.

'Because I do, Claire. I do. I'm the father. I have rights, too.'

Claire felt as if she'd been holding herself erect for days now. Ever since the pregnancy had been confirmed. She had to be strong. She had to be. There were so many decisions still to make.

'I'd hate to trample on your rights, Campbell, but trust me—' sarcasm laced her voice '—it just isn't that simple.'

'Sure it is. You either love this baby or you don't.'

'You think I don't love this baby?' Claire felt the tears gather and was stung by his words.

'I don't know, Claire. I don't understand any of this.'

'Come with me,' she snapped, and marched down the hallway, flinging her mother's door open. 'Look at her, Campbell. Look at her.' Tears streamed unchecked down her face. 'What's your diagnosis?'

'I don't know. I assumed it was cancer.'

Claire's brittle laugh echoed around the room.

'Cancer? Oh, Campbell, cancer would be so simple. No, my mother has Huntington's disease.'

Claire watched through her tears as realisation dawned

on the face of the man she loved. 'That's right, Campbell, take a good look. This could be me in ten or twenty years. It could be our child. You want me to inflict this on our baby, because I sure as hell don't. So don't tell me I don't love this child.'

She ran from the room, sobbing, brushing past a stunned Campbell. He stood stock-still, trying to analyse the information she'd just thrown at him. He searched his grey matter for what he could remember about Huntington's.

It was a degenerative disease of the central nervous system. It slowly renders the sufferers incapable of normal body functions leading to premature death. And it was genetic.

So Claire could have inherited it. And so could the baby.

CHAPTER NINE

THINGS were starting to make sense now, Campbell thought as he took some time to sort through the jumble of thoughts spinning around in his head. Bits of the crazy puzzle were falling into place. This was what it had been about all along. This was why she'd pushed him away.

When he joined her a few minutes later she was sitting in a chair, her eyes red and puffy. She looked so miserable he ached to hold her. But now was not the time for that. It was finally time to clear the air.

'Are you telling me you also have it?'

'Not so cut and dried, is it?'

'You think I'm going to run away because of this? You think I'm going to dump you because of this, like Shane did? I'm not him, Claire.'

'You told me to my face that you would think twice about bringing a child into this world if there was a history of genetic illness. Well, that's exactly what's happened here, Campbell. So pardon me if I got the impression that you wouldn't be interested.'

'Just because I said I'd think twice, it doesn't mean I'd abandon you because it's happened. That CF couple planned their second baby knowing full well the possible consequences. This is different. It was an accident.'

'Is it different because of that or different because it's you?'

'Claire, look, all that matters to me right now is our baby. And you. I love you. That's all that matters—we'll deal with the rest together. I know we can make this work.'

He loved her. Those three little words slammed right into her solar plexus. Her heart wanted to take flight and soar—he loved her. She wanted to go to him and tell him she loved him, too, but she held back.

She couldn't confide her love until after the test. If it was negative, she could rejoice in his love and share hers in return. If it was positive, he must never know how she felt.

Claire didn't want to burden him with an invalid and watch his love turn to sympathy and pity. They would always have to have a relationship because of their child, but she would never allow him to be an intimate part of her life if it turned out she had the disease.

'You have no idea,' she said quietly, shaking her head, quashing the elation she'd felt at his declaration.

'Explain it to me, then. I am a doctor.' She rose from the chair, still shaking her head.

'It's got nothing to do with the extent of your medical knowledge. It's to do with the reality of the disease. In ten years I've watched my father become an old man. I've seen his heart break little by little and I know, I just know, that somewhere inside the shell that is now my mother she's seen it, too. I don't want that to be us. I don't want it to be you. Why do you think I've pushed you away all this time?'

'So you've had the predictive test?'

'No.'

'What do you mean—no?' Campbell could hardly believe his ears.

Claire sighed. 'It's not so easy, Campbell. Mum was diagnosed ten years ago, and from that moment on I lost my mother. She gave up. Just took to her bed and waited to die. I was so determined that wasn't going to be me. I refuse to let this disease define me, as my mother has. I'd rather not know than live my life under a death sentence.'

'A simple blood test, Claire, that's all it takes.'

'I know that, Campbell. You think I don't know that? It sounds so simple but the reality is terrifying. What if it's positive?'

'What if it's negative?'

'It's all right for you. You've got what you wanted.'

'What do I want, Claire?' he asked softly.

'You've got me in a position where you have a hold over me. You probably planned this all along. You probably used defective condoms.'

Campbell laughed. It felt good to get some relief from the intensity of their conversation.

'This isn't a joke for me. This is my life.'

'I love you, Claire, and I understand you're scared.'

'Scared?' His love and reassurance soothed the hysteria that threatened. 'I'm terrified, Campbell. Do you know what it's like to live day by day with this hanging over your head? Every time you drop something or forget something, you wonder, Is this it? Do I have it? And then having to watch as it ravages your mother, wondering all the time if this is going to be me.'

'So get tested. Stop the guesswork.'

'Relax, Campbell. I'm seeing my geneticist in a few days—I've already made the appointment. I know I have to take the test for the baby's sake. I know that. I'm just…still in a state of shock about the pregnancy and I'm scared. I think I'm already experiencing some symptoms of Huntington's.'

Campbell felt fear clutch his heart. Claire was scared and he wanted to comfort and support her through this. But how could he do that when he was so terrified himself? Frightened for Claire and for the baby. He loved her and he just couldn't bear the thought of the woman he loved going through such mental anguish.

'If you test positive—' Campbell's voice shook '—then we can have the baby tested.'

'And if it's positive?' Claire shuddered at the thought.

'Claire, this disease isn't like CF. Its onset doesn't start until later, right? So...medicine, genetics, is moving ahead in leaps and bounds. If the baby carries the gene, it'll be, what...another thirty, forty years before it's symptomatic, right? By then they'll be able to selectively remove genes that cause diseases. They've already mapped DNA, it's only a matter of time before genetic illnesses are obliterated.'

Too late for her, though. Claire shook her head, quashing the self-pity as quickly as it had appeared. He had a point. She felt a ray of hope rising inside her. Claire used her hands to swipe the tears from her face.

Genetic advances were happening daily. In the future it would be acknowledged that this period in medicine had been second only to the era when penicillin had been discovered.

'You're right.' She smiled a watery smile.

'I know.' He grinned and they laughed despite the circumstances.

'I love you, Claire. No...' He held up his hand and her interruption died on her lips. 'I know it's not reciprocated. I know there's too much stuff happening in your life at the moment to think about loving me back, but I need you to know how I feel. I'm telling you because I want you to draw strength and determination from my love. Let it make you stronger to face the next few days and weeks and whatever they hold. Just lean on me.'

Claire felt tears well in her eyes again at the sweetness and sincerity of his words. He was right. With his love behind her, she could face anything. She could face the future and fight for herself and her baby if she needed to.

He was, of course, wrong about his love not being reciprocated, but Claire knew it was wise to keep her own counsel. Her life suddenly felt in limbo, dependent on the results of a blood test. Would she be a winner or loser in this cruel genetic lottery?

Three days later, Claire and Campbell sat in the waiting room of Dr Robyn Laidley. Claire battled waves of nausea. Was it morning sickness or extreme nervousness? Claire hadn't been able to stomach breakfast. In fact, food had lost all its appeal over the last few days. Eating was something that was purely functional—she forced herself to do it for the sake of the baby.

Campbell shifted in his chair and smiled at her. She looked away and he squeezed her hands, knowing she was nervous and wanting to comfort her. They felt cold and he instinctively rubbed them between his.

The phone buzzed and the receptionist answered it, murmuring quietly.

'Claire West,' she announced in a clear voice, standing to direct the way.

Campbell and Claire took the indicated seats in the large, modern room and waited in silence for a few minutes. The door behind the desk opened.

'Claire.' Dr Laidley greeted her as she entered. 'It's been a long time.'

'Hello, Robyn.'

It may have been ten years, but the geneticist who had played such a pivotal part in Claire's life all those years ago looked exactly the same.

She'd forgotten how tall the doctor was, almost Amazonian in stature, with softly curled red hair only now showing the signs that she had entered the fifth decade of her life. She wore fashionable glasses that made her appear even younger.

'You must be Dr Deane.' Her eyes twinkled as she extended her hand.

'Campbell,' he said, shaking her hand. 'Don't tell me hospital gossip reaches all the way down here.'

'No, not really.' She laughed. 'I have my sources.'

Campbell's laughter grated on Claire's already stretched nerves. She knew they were just being friendly but she wanted to yell at them to shut up. It didn't seem right to laugh in this office where she'd only ever heard bad news.

'I'm a little surprised to see you, Claire.' Robyn got down to business. 'Last time I saw you, you were adamant I wouldn't be seeing you again.'

'To be honest, I'd really rather not be here, but...my circumstances have changed.'

'Oh? How so? Are you experiencing symptoms?'

'I...could be...' Actually admitting the possibility out loud to Robyn was terrifying.

'I get the feeling there's more,' Robyn prompted.

Claire couldn't speak. Weren't symptoms enough? How could she tell Robyn about the baby when she'd stood in this very office years before and insisted she'd never burden a child with her mutant genes?

'Claire is pregnant,' Campbell stated.

'Ah...I see.' Robyn removed her glasses and placed one earpiece between her teeth, sucking thoughtfully. 'So, your symptoms have been...?'

'Oh...um...some clumsiness, forgetfulness.'

'For how long?'

'A month, maybe a little longer.' Claire's brow creased trying to concentrate on the facts.

'And you're how many weeks pregnant?'

'Nine.'

Claire could practically see the brain cells working be-
nd the geneticist's eyes. They were busily forming im-
essions, gathering data and analysing it.

'So these might not be symptoms at all, at least not of
e disease?'

'I suppose…' said Claire, sounding unconvinced.

'It could just be the pregnancy. You both must know
enty of women who complain of an appalling memory
hen they're expecting. That hormonal haze is a killer.'

'Very common,' Campbell agreed.

'So. You want to be tested.'

'No.'

'Claire?' Confusion furrowed Robyn's brow.

'I'm here to have the test, yes. But do I want to take it?
o. Not one iota.'

Robyn peered over her glasses at the two of them.
ampbell felt her shrewd gaze weighing him up and won-
red what she was thinking. Was she thinking what a sorry
ir they were? Why two people, supposedly in a relation-
ip and about to have a child, looked so damned misera-
e?

'Campbell wants you to take the test,' she stated.

Neither of them spoke, and Campbell felt his misery in-
nsify. Great. Now Robyn was going to think him some
nd of ogre.

'You do know, Campbell, that the implications of this
st are potentially quite awful for Claire? She needs to be
motionally prepared as much as possible before she con-
nts to this.'

'Robyn.' Campbell half sighed, half groaned. 'I'm well
ware of that. And, believe me, if this was just about her
d me, I wouldn't be pushing. Good Lord,' he said, raking
s hand through his hair, pushing his floppy fringe away,
don't care about the bloody test! I love Claire, disease

or no disease.' Frustration welled inside him and added a husky quality to his voice. 'But there's another person involved now—my child.'

Robyn was quiet again, tapping her glasses against her pursed lips. The silence stretched between them. 'Why don't I start right from the beginning? We'll get a family history from both of you and I can work out a pedigree, and from there we can assess the risks to your baby.'

'That's kind of pointless, isn't it, Robyn?' Claire stated quietly. 'I mean, if I have the gene then my baby has a fifty per cent chance of inheriting it, too. That's right, isn' it?'

'Yes,' Robyn admitted, 'but now we can do special tests and actually find out the baby's status. You'd be much better equipped with that kind of information to make decisions. There have been some interesting advances in this area in the past decade.'

'Can they cure it yet?'

'No.'

'Well, that's the only advance that matters to me.'

'Maybe some more counselling will prepare you bette should you carry the gene.'

'Can you ever really be prepared for that?'

Robyn was savvy enough to know a rhetorical questio when it came her way. She stayed silent.

'Frankly,' Claire sighed, 'I think it'll be a relief. As muc as I've tried to ignore it, deny it—it's there. It's alway there. I've lived my life refusing to let this disease defin me, but I think it's time to stop driving myself crazy wit what-ifs. And I need to know for the baby's sake. Ye Campbell really wants me to take the test. But I need know, too. I need to be prepared.'

'Yes,' Robyn said after a short while, 'I think you' right. Very sensible. I'll write out the lab form.'

Claire watched as Robyn scribbled on a piece of paper. She suddenly felt better than she had in weeks. She felt like she was taking control of her life again. OK, the result was in the lap of the gods, but as she squeezed the hand of the man beside her she knew his love would help her through.

'Now, some things have changed since I last saw you. As a consequence of the Huntington gene being isolated in 1993, we can now do direct gene testing.'

'I've been reading up on this. You look for a repeat in the DNA sequence, right?' said Campbell.

'Yes, we identify the fourth chromosome and look for a series of repeated units of information known as CAG repeats. We all have these, but in the general population you find less than twenty-nine CAG repeats. In affected individuals the CAG repeats number between forty and fifty-five, sometimes higher.'

'What if you have more than twenty-nine but less than forty?' asked Claire.

'Well, that falls into a grey area. I can tell you that people with twenty-nine to thirty-five CAG repeats have never been documented with the disease.'

'So,' said Claire, wanting to clarify the technical information, 'it all depends on how many of these CAG repeats I have. Right?'

'Right.'

'How long until the test results come back?' she asked.

'Two weeks. We'll make an appointment for you in a fortnight and we can discuss the results.'

'Can't you just ring me with them?'

'No. If they come back with elevated CAG repeats, I want to be able to tell you face to face. It's not the kind of information I want to give you over the phone.'

'I don't think I can wait two weeks,' Claire said.

'That's understandable,' Robyn agreed. 'But that's the way it is. Look…I know it's easy for me to say, but try and use these next two weeks thinking positively. And you need to take better care of yourself, Claire. I'm sorry to say this but you look like hell.'

Robyn was right, Claire decided, assessing her features critically in the mirror above the handbasin in the public toilets on the way to the laboratory. She smiled at herself and winced at how wan she looked. She did look like hell!

Campbell accompanied her to the lab for her blood test. Claire thought he was probably escorting her to prevent her from bolting than for any other reason, but she was grateful for his presence anyway. Whatever his motive.

As the needle pierced her skin Claire felt her doubts and fears return. What if she had the gene? How would she cope with the awful knowledge that she had a terminal degenerative illness?

Campbell saw the fear in her eyes and tried to imagine how terrible it must be confronting the reality of Huntington's. He couldn't. It must be too awful for words. He loved her more at this moment than he ever had, his heart swelling with pride. This was extreme bravery. He squeezed her hand and she clutched his harder.

'You don't have it,' he said, looking into her panicky eyes.

'How do you know?' she whispered, wanting to believe him, wishing she possessed his assuredness.

'I just do.'

'I wish I could be so sure.' Her voice trembled.

'Positive. We have to be positive.'

Claire nodded, not trusting her voice as she held the cotton ball over the puncture site in the crook of her arm. The nurse fixed it with surgical tape.

Campbell drove Claire home, reciting his positive-thinking mantra while she tried to ignore her dread and the motion of the car and concentrate on not throwing up.

'I've been thinking,' he said as he turned off the engine, 'Robyn has a point about looking after yourself. You do look… Well, you've looked better.'

'Gee, thanks,' she said, feeling less queasy now the car was stationary.

'Maybe you should take the next couple weeks off work. Eat, sleep and pamper yourself a bit. Come and stay with me. I'll treat you like a queen.'

It sounded like bliss. A fortnight being cocooned in his love and attention. But she couldn't allow such intimacy yet. She didn't trust herself not to blurt out her feelings, and she was determined to keep them secret at all costs. She needed him to keep thinking she didn't love him because once she told him, there would be no going back.

'I appreciate your concern.' She smiled gratefully. 'But I'll go mad if I'm not occupied. I really need work to keep my mind off the test. I promise I'll take care of myself…really. And there's Mum to consider…'

'All right, then. I don't agree with you but I understand.'

He smiled at her and ran his index finger down her cheek. Silence filled the car as their gazes locked. He placed his hand on her flat stomach. Claire felt her insides contract followed by a flare of sexual desire. It had been a while since they had been intimate. The sudden need to feel him deep inside her shook her to the core.

'Promise me you'll look after yourself and my baby,' he said huskily.

'I promise,' she said, and crossed her heart.

Campbell found the next two weeks interminable. They dragged by, and he could only imagine how much worse it must be for Claire. He ran into her quite a lot at work, and was cheered by how much better she was looking.

No one could accuse her of having that glow that so many pregnant women had but she looked healthy. She was laughing more and she seemed to be eating almost every time he saw her.

Campbell was saddened that he was denied access to her changing body. He desperately wanted to see the differences in her shape as his baby grew inside her. It wasn't anything sexual, more primal. This was his baby and he wanted to be there to see her stomach blossom and her breasts become fuller and feel the first stirring of foetal movement. Staying away was the hardest thing he'd ever had to do.

He refused to think about the results in any other than a positive way. He couldn't explain why he felt so certain, he just did. And the times his thoughts did wander down the negative track, he knew it wouldn't matter to him. You love for better or worse, right? In sickness and in health?

All he knew was that he wanted to be with her and their baby. The test results would decide his fate, too. They both had a lot riding on them.

It was Friday. The appointment with Robyn Laidley was on Monday. Claire, who had managed quite well to keep herself busy this last fortnight, just couldn't distract her mind from the imminent results.

She took a phone call from Brian Craven, updating her on baby Charlotte's progress. She'd had the breathing tube removed yesterday and had done well overnight. Charlotte had really turned the corner. Claire decided to go up and see her. At least it would be a distraction—a happy one at that.

Campbell was there when she arrived, holding the baby

and blowing raspberries on her tiny fingers. Claire instinctively cradled her still flat stomach. He would be a terrific
father.

'Claire,' said Lex. 'Come and hold our precious girl.'

Claire joined the circle, acutely aware of Campbell's intimate stare. She held out her arms for Campbell to place
Charlotte in them. Their gazes locked, a heat rising between
them. Claire moistened her dry lips and watched
Campbell's eyes dilate with desire.

'Hasn't she grown?' Lex chatted away obliviously.

Claire had trouble focusing her attention on the baby.
Seeing Campbell reminded her of the desperation she felt
about her situation. Worse than that, it seemed to be pushing them together. She should be discouraging this sudden
heat between them, but Monday loomed large and he was
the only other person who knew what she was going
through.

'I actually managed to try a breastfeed with her this
morning. She's amazed everyone. She's our little fighter,'
gushed the proud mother.

Claire smiled and nodded and mumbled the odd appropriate reply, but as wonderful as baby Charlotte's progress
was she was tuned into a different wavelength.

Campbell and Claire left together, chatting inanely about
Charlotte. They got into the lift, and their conversation pe-
tered out. They stood side by side, close but not touching.

'Come back to my house for the weekend.' Campbell
spoke into the silence.

'OK,' she agreed.

They smiled at each other, and he took her hand and
pressed a kiss on her palm. The look in her eyes told Claire
he was about to slam her against the wall and ravage her.
She felt her breath quicken in anticipation, but the lift
dinged and the doors open and people crowded in.

Claire couldn't explain it. She just had to see Campbell. As much as she knew she should stay away, he was the only person who understood. She had the weekend off and she couldn't bear the thought of having all that time on her hands. She needed to forget everything this weekend, and two days in his company would be a very pleasant distraction.

Claire's father was pleased when she rang him to inform him of her plans. He'd sensed she was struggling with something but had tactfully decided not to push. He knew his daughter would tell him when the time was right. He was relieved that she was getting out of the house for a while. She'd given up too much of her life helping him with Mary.

Claire and Campbell travelled in his car to the apartment in silence. Their thoughts were separate but similar. They both knew that destiny was running their lives and there was nothing they could do to stop it. The sense of impending fate hung over them like a thundercloud. They needed each other to navigate a way through the next couple of days.

Campbell pushed the door open and pulled Claire into the room and into his arms.

'I'm sorry. I tried to stay away,' he whispered, and he held her and murmured words of love. He felt so helpless. What did you say to someone who was facing demons few people faced? All he could offer her was the solace of his embrace, as she had offered hers when he had needed it. He hoped it was enough for this moment.

She pulled back a little so she could see his face.

'Me, too. I'm sorry. I'm not being fair to you…'

'Shh. It doesn't matter. I love you. I've always love

you.' He brushed a strand of hair from her forehead and kissed her there gently.

'I know,' she whispered. 'I wish it was enough.'

'It is, Claire. It is.'

She shut her eyes and let herself believe it for a moment, but deep down she knew. If the blood test revealed that she had the gene, love just wasn't going to cut it. She'd push him so far away, drive him if necessary, that he'd never be able to get back. Never want to. She wouldn't have the man she loved sacrifice his life for her, like her father had done for her mother. She loved Campbell too much to put him through that ordeal.

But those were issues they'd be tackling soon enough. This weekend was about distraction. What would be on Monday would be.

Claire kissed him and it *was* enough for now. More than enough. She felt the reaction shudder through his body and pressed herself closer to him. She needed to be closer to him than she'd ever been.

They tore at each other's clothes, rushing, stumbling, fumbling towards the bed. Finally naked, they fell onto the bed and into each other. Claire was impatient for his touch and felt tears spill from her eyes as he buried himself in her and cried out her name. Yes. This was where he belonged. Where she belonged.

Claire wanted to freeze this moment in time and stay like this for eternity…part of each other. Connected. Not just physically but spiritually. Bodies and souls joined.

But the rhythm began to take over, pounding through her head and throbbing in her veins. The primal tempo of physical bonding that could not be denied, like an itch you just had to scratch. Claire revelled in it, welcomed each thrust, urged him deeper until she wasn't sure where her cries ended and his began.

*   *   *

Claire slept peacefully for the first night in weeks. The usual elusive fragments of dreams about babies and test results, which haunted her, waking her in a cold sweat, were blissfully absent. If only for that, the night was worth it.

They woke late on Saturday morning. The familiar nausea assailed her the second she opened her eyes. Claire remembered they hadn't eaten last night as she ran her hand over her stomach and pleaded with the baby to give her a break. It was no use, it was only a matter of time.

Campbell rolled towards her, snuggling into her side. 'Hmm,' he murmured, nuzzling her ear.

'Ugh!' she muttered, dashing from the bed into the *en suite*, retching into the toilet.

'Oh, Claire!' Campbell squatted beside her and rubbed her back. 'Are you all right? What can I do?'

'Strong, black tea. Two sugars,' she croaked. 'Dry toast—' She broke off as another wave of nausea caused her to retch again.

Claire stayed clinging to the toilet for a few minutes until she was sure the nausea had passed. She emptied her bladder, brushed her teeth and walked weakly back to bed.

Campbell arrived with a tray as she was pulling the sheet over herself. He passed her the steaming mug of tea and she sipped it gratefully between mouthfuls of toast. After she'd eaten the breakfast, Campbell took the tray and she lay back down on her side beneath the sheet.

He joined her in bed, curling around her, spoon-fashion. They lay in silence for a while.

'Claire?'

'Hmm?'

'About Monday.'

'No. No plans. We'll get the result then we'll go from

there.' Claire didn't want to argue this weekend and she certainly didn't want to be reminded about Monday.

A phone ringing cut off any potential conversation, and Claire realised it was her mobile. She dug around in her handbag for it.

'Hello?' Claire lay back against Campbell, his lips nuzzled her neck.

'Claire?'

'Speaking.'

'This is Robyn. Robyn Laidley.'

Claire's heart skipped a beat. She lifted herself up on her elbow, displacing Campbell.

'What's wrong?' she asked ominously.

'Nothing, nothing. Honestly. It's just that…well, I came into the office today to catch up on some paperwork and your results are here.'

'Oh?' Claire was sure her heart had now actually stopped.

'I know I don't usually ring but…it's twenty-two, Claire. Twenty-two.'

'Twenty-two,' Claire repeated.

'Twenty-two CAG repeats. You don't have the gene, Claire.'

'Twenty-two,' she repeated again.

'Yes, you don't have the gene!'

'I don't.'

'No.'

'So…the baby?'

'Doesn't either.'

Claire felt tears course down her cheeks. She was free. She didn't have Huntington's. Her baby didn't either. She was really free. Robyn continued to speak but Claire took none of it in. She was free.

'What's the matter? Who is it?' Campbell sat up, concern

creasing his brow as Claire dropped the phone in her lap. 'What about the baby?' he asked.

'You want to know what my favourite number is, Campbell?' Claire grinned a silly juvenile grin and her heart sang as she kissed him. 'Twenty-two. I'm going to get a new number plate for my car with twenty-two on it.'

'I don't understand. Twenty-two?' he said, wiping the tears flowing thick and fast down her face.

'That was Robyn. Twenty-two.'

Claire watched as realisation dawned on his face.

'CAG repeats? Are we talking about CAG repeats?'

'I don't have it, Campbell,' she said. 'I don't have Huntington's.'

She threw herself into his arms, feeling lighter and giddier and younger than she had in years. She wanted to dash out into the street and yell it to the world.

'So the baby…' he said, pushing her away slightly by the hips.

'Our beautiful baby doesn't have it either. Oh, Campbell, isn't it wonderful?'

'It's the best news ever,' he agreed, kissing her again. 'I love you, I love you, I love you,' he said, dropping kisses all over her face.

'You couldn't possibly love me as much as I love you,' she said between kisses.

He stilled and cradled her face in his hands, suddenly serious.

'You…you do?'

'Of course, you silly man. I think I've always loved you. I just didn't realise it and then when I did realise I couldn't tell you…not till I knew the result anyway. I would never have admitted it if I'd been positive. I love you too much to burden you with an invalid.'

'When will you get it through your head,' he growled

and kissed her nose, 'that I don't care about that? I've never cared about it. When you love someone, it's in sickness and in health.'

'I know that, but I still would never have allowed it.'

'I would have worn you down. You'd have been so sick of the sight of me you'd have given in just to shut me up.'

She laughed and they hugged and kissed again, passion escalating from their joy.

'No. Stop,' said Campbell, extricating himself and leaping out of bed. He started to dress.

'Why?' She pouted at him.

'We're going to go and buy you the biggest, most expensive ring we can find. We're getting married. As soon as possible. No arguments.'

'As if I could argue with you, you obstinate man.' Claire laughed and rose from the bed, going straight into his arms.

'I love you, Claire West.'

'I love you, Campbell Deane.'

'Let's get hitched.'

And they did.

EPILOGUE

CLAIRE and Campbell stared down at their sleeping newborn daughter. Baby Mary was blissfully unaware of their rapt attention.

'I wish Mum could have seen her,' she whispered. Mary had died three months before.

'She knows,' he said, pulling her close.

They stood and stared at their daughter, lost in their own thoughts.

'I can't imagine life without her. Can you?' asked Campbell.

'Absolutely not,' said Claire, stroking Mary's cheek.

'Just think, if I hadn't been so persistent, so—'

'Obstinate. Stubborn. Infuriating. Single-minded,' Claire interrupted, a smile on her face.

'Yes.' He laughed. 'All those things. Mary wouldn't be here today.'

'Yeah right,' Claire snorted. 'She'd be here all right—just a bit later, that's all. I know you well enough to know you'd have never given up.'

A knock at the door interrupted their conversation.

'I'll go,' he whispered, and kissed Claire's cheek. He signed for a rectangular package addressed to Claire.

'It's for you,' he said, as she joined him.

Claire knew what it was just from the shape, and eagerly tore open the cardboard to reveal her brand-new personalised number plates.

The word TWENTY-TWO gleamed up at her in shiny red letters. Claire laughed and showed Campbell. He grinned at her.

'C'mon, baby,' he said, 'let's go put them on.'

4 FREE

BOOKS AND A SURPRISE GIFT!

We would like to take this opportunity to thank you for reading this Mills & Boon® book by offering you the chance to take FOUR more specially selected titles from the Medical Romance™ series absolutely FREE! We're also making this offer to introduce you to the benefits of the Reader Service™—

- ★ **FREE home delivery**
- ★ **FREE gifts and competitions**
- ★ **FREE monthly Newsletter**
- ★ **Exclusive Reader Service offers**
- ★ **Books available before they're in the shops**

Accepting these FREE books and gift places you under no obligation to buy, you may cancel at any time, even after receiving your free shipment. Simply complete your details below and return the entire page to the address below. You don't even need a stamp!

YES! Please send me 4 free Medical Romance books and a surprise gift. I understand that unless you hear from me, I will receive 6 superb new titles every month for just £2.75 each, postage and packing free. I am under no obligation to purchase any books and may cancel my subscription at any time. The free books and gift will be mine to keep in any case.

M5ZED

Ms/Mrs/Miss/Mr ....Initials ....
BLOCK CAPITALS PLEASE

Surname ....

Address ....

....

....:..................Postcode...................

Send this whole page to:
UK: FREEPOST CN81, Croydon, CR9 3WZ